Everything Must Go La JohnJoseph

I T N A
P R E S S

La JohnJoseph © copyright 2014
All rights reserved.
ISBN: 978-0-9912196-4-3
Library of Congress Control Number: 2013954364
Printed in the United States of America.

Cover art: Stevie Hanley © copyright 2014
Cover design: Christopher Stoddard

ITNA
PRESS

This book is the song of my sisters, dedicated with gratitude to Our Holy Mother.

Acknowledgments

To my dearest friends: Sophie, Max, Stevie, Jordan, Anna, Nicola, Evelyn and Tucker for their limitless encouragement and knowing kindnesses. To my siblings whom I love unreservedly, my nieces who are the pearls in my tiara, and my Mother, of whom I only ever grow fonder. To Sarah and Charles for believing in my writing and helping me to better understand what it was I was trying to say. To Bruce for his thorough engagement with the text and his illuminating feedback. To Chris at ITNA for making this book a reality. And to Ami for the Turkish snowflakes and the Thai crabs, the ferris wheel, the old red car and the hirsch; bottle top.

Part One:
Going, Going, Gone

Plus One

At first I couldn't comprehend the flowers that began to bud amongst the thick evergreen leaves of the stubby shrub down at the bottom of my childhood garden. In my thirteen years the plant had never flowered, and now here it was, finally aflame with blood-red buds. As they opened, they sprouted nasty little tongues that spewed forth, extending longer, revealing themselves not fleshy or muscular, but rather of man-made fibres.

Shredded polyester pants, besplattered spaghetti-strap T-shirts, odd shoes, stained sports jackets, bloody jockstraps and a pair of torn schoolboy's trousers; the clothes of murder victims, all hocked up by the plant in the course of a few days and deposited, mucus covered, onto the sun-parched lawn. I watched, spellbound and horrified as the plant grew at an exaggerated rate, doubling in size every other day.

Then came the bodies, eviscerated, strangulated, castrated, rotting, mangled and contorted, expelled by the retching of the foliage, attracting armies of insects almost immediately. The smell was terrible, and ominous, because the murder bush was not only mourning for killings of the past, but also announcing the future. The murder bush bloomed to celebrate a forthcoming crime, the murder bush was psychic, the murder bush was waking up to anoint me.

There were just two things in the world that I loved. Sisterhood, my golden retriever, and Myra, the one-eyed stuffed elephant who sat at the end of my bed. Both had been with me since infancy, I had grown up with them, we were all thirteen years old. Both of them had witnessed my desecration at the hands of my father.

On some sunny day I don't remember, before she left without explanation, my mother must have popped Myra into my cradle (back when she still had both eyes) and laughed, as Sisterhood jumped up excitedly to get a better look at squirming little pupal me. The sunshine undoubtedly poured in through the window and into my nursery, all pink and smelling of fresh paint. Sisterhood quite probably comically gave chase to a noisy bluebottle.

"A-coo, a-coo, a-goo, goo, gah," it's likely I said, as my father stubbed a cigarette out on my seven-year-old brother, Tom. Later in life, James Dean told me that he liked Marlon Brando to put cigarettes out on him when they were fucking. I don't know if that was the archetype my father was mining, but reflecting on his character now, it doesn't seem so far off.

I grew up without a name. I didn't attend Mass, since the world had torn itself to shreds and I was living in a lesion. At a certain point, and no one was quite sure when exactly, the little green wheels had fallen off the carriage of time. One day, quite unannounced, a sphere had appeared in the sky. It hung there, suspended over the city of Jerusalem for a moment, so massive it could be seen worldwide, and then silently, dreadfully, it dropped (like the ball in Times Square on New Year's

Eve, but without the brouhaha). I can just about remember sitting on my father's shoulders, in a wheat field, gazing up forlornly at this beautiful mystery, watching it descend and disappear below the horizon.

Some say it was the bomb, some say it was an alien landing, some say it was God—I think it was the not knowing that drove people to such fits of savage paranoia. A little later the hands dropped off Big Ben, and the Great Wall of China wrapped herself python-like around North Dakota; time and space handed in their resignations, took early retirement, and moved to the country to rear rare-breed lambs and campaign for fair trade.

A little later the Earth sucked the oceans inside of herself, and great geysers of scalding water erupted where Rome and Brisbane once stood—there can be no fixity in the face of a flood. A little later, a great wave of St. Vitus's Dance swept the globe; though strangely, only heads of state were affected, and they danced themselves to death in a manner horrible but ever so entertaining, leaving the world leaderless. And so this is the world I inherited, Lamb of God that I am.

I often daydreamed about my childhood as I entered my adolescence, or rather, as it entered me. When I found my teenage self travelling the world, in conditions of psychedelic depravity, I would occasionally smile to myself in reverie of those halcyon days I called my childhood; when it was always spring, when screams for mercy perpetually hung in the air, when the postman always had a cheery letter from Granny, and the smell of burnt hair permeated the cottage. (At seventeen, finding myself somewhere in Poland, drenched in sewage, wrestling a crocodile, and reflecting on my youth, I would sigh whimsically to myself, "Alas! Long gone are those icing sugar-dusted days!")

Of the child that I was then, what can I tell you? Father was a meth head, which is painfully dull, but painfully true. My brother Tom hanged himself, unceremoniously, on the day of his nineteenth birthday. Sisterhood, though she had practically raised me ever since mother disappeared, was undoubtedly becoming skittish in her golden years. I was thirteen then and everything was changing; the gauntlet was being laid down before me. The very ground beneath my feet was turning molten, the tectonic plates on which the world was served slipped and slid as they would, I was born just in time to see the murder bush blossom and the world die, and the murder bush blossom.

Against the buzzing of the flies, our parish priest stood in the garden, blessing the wildly enlarged plant with holy water. Weeping over the regurgitated corpses, he looked particularly grieved by a ruby-red high-heeled pump that he seemed to recognize.

"Everybody has a heart," the priest said, misty-eyed, "except some people."

A secretary on her way to the office (which everyone knew meant whorehouse) had been set upon by a particularly tempestuous dog that shredded her to, well, shreds, out of pure blood lust and sunstroke. This shoe was apparently all that remained of her. Everyone said that it was a terrible thing to happen to anyone; even a whore didn't deserve to be torn limb from limb by a rabid hound. Even in death the poor woman seemed irresistible to canine sensibilities. Sisterhood as well began collecting tidbits of gristle formerly belonging to the various sinews of the secretary, from amongst the exudations of the murder bush.

From this collection, I reassembled a part of her left hand and set up a little altar for her, adorned with paper flowers made from pages torn from a pristine copy of *Cosmopolitan*, which I had discovered amongst the cadavers. 'Are there *really* that many ways to please your man?' I wondered to myself, as I virginally leafed through the pages in the late afternoon sunlight. I thought hard about the secretary and I decided that her name was probably Francesca; I made her a saint and kept her hand as a most holy relic.

I had many powerfully erotic dreams about Saint Francesca, as thirteen-year-olds are wont to do. I dreamt that Saint Francesca was looking for her hand, that she came into my bedroom and touched me all over—sexually—with her bloody stump of an arm. She was covered in scars like tattoos. She had been sewn up by the Virgin Mary in Heaven, but her cunt was still open. The touch of her stump felt magical, passionate, and she played games with me by pretending not to know where her hand was hidden.

"Oh, maybe it's in here," she said, chuckling and plunging into my underwear.

Saint Francesca ate me out, and I came hard in her face as she searched me for her missing limb. Her caress was like a snake's, muscular, soothing, lithe, knowing; she raised me up. I awoke and my father was fucking me. Well, not even fucking me, just holding my jaw tightly and rubbing his half-hard dick on my pussy.

In a time of such endless ritual atrocities, an epoch when fresh bodies were strung from lamp posts daily, when planes dropped out of the sky hourly, when whole towns slid into the sea with such monotonous frequency, I could well be forgiven for forgetting the specifics of how my drug-addicted father, psychopathic with fear and loss, raped me with such malice that I barely survived. I could well be.

My recollections have shattered. I remember that Myra was there, useless stuffed elephant that she was, and that she was talking me through it, part life coach, part post-traumatic stress counsellor, alternately suggesting coping techniques and mocking me with streetwalker sass. I remember that I tried to twist, I tried to turn, I tried to beg, I tried to loosen my father's grip, I tried to scream, and I prayed to Saint Francesca that her severed hand might reanimate and rip my father's dick from his torso. No such luck. His eyes glowed feline in the darkness of my bedroom and spilt luminosity over the dopey pink plush cushions I had scattered about my bed in the hope of setting the scene for some more magical encounter with (maybe) Freddy, the red-haired boy in geography class who everyone called a faggot.

Every day, religiously, at lunchtime, people hit Freddy in the head with their lunchboxes, until his face was practically deformed and he was always bleeding from some huge gash. He looked like Christ pelted by tin lunch pails to me, assailed daily by a merciless onslaught of Tupperware about his head like a halo. I wanted him. I wanted him to come up to my room and sit on my bed and let me sew up his cheek and run my fingers through the blood in his eyebrows, congealed like chocolate syrup on an unloved dessert.

They say that in moments of great trauma the mind breaks away from the body, that she get gets up from the sofa to change the channel, flips through a few made-for-TV movies and a quiz show or two, before a soap opera or a shampoo commercial catches her eye and she settles back in, unthinking. Unexpectedly, Freddy is who caught my eye, and was onto whom I latched as the last remaining recognizable fragments of life were ground in a pestle into dust as my father tore out my virginity.

When it was done, my father went to the gas station to buy a celebratory liter of ginger ale, the sugar-free kind (he has type 2 diabetes). In a stone-cold daze, I collected the pieces of my body, picked them up one by one, and stitched myself back together just as I had done with St. Francesca's hand (for all the good that did me). There was silence. I sat thinking about Freddy and his thing for old movie stars. There was one specific old black-and-white Katharine Hepburn film he had screened on a wet Wednesday afternoon when the class was bored and aimless, after Mrs. Moore the geography teacher was assassinated by pre-teen terrorists. Screwball comedies. It's really no wonder everyone called him a faggot, is it? Irritatingly, I could not recall the name of the movie. You know the one? She's trying to seduce a palaeontologist, but she accidentally pulls his brontosaurus skeleton down on herself? Whatever was it called?

"*The Philadelphia Story*," suggested Myra, face down in the shagpile, besmirched with a streak of blood.

"That's not it," I mumbled back, quite sure she was incorrect.

Myra tried again. "*The African Queen*?"

"No," I growled. "This one was in black and white."

"Erm, *His Girl Friday*?"

"Oh shu-ut u-p!" I hissed at her insistence, "Katharine Hepburn isn't even *in* that movie!"

Musing, maybe staggering a little, I made my way outside, into the garden, drawn perhaps by the stench of the now massive murder bush, which had grown to smell so sweet to me. It was a purple night with barely any trace of color to be witnessed under the saturated womb of the moon. The shrubbery and its gruesome vomitings had become epic. The bush had greedily consumed half the garden, feasting on all the other plant life. Currently it was at rest.

"Diana," came a whisper.

I instinctively turned toward the bush, the voice seemingly emanating from within the bosom of its blossoms.

"Me?" I asked, hand to my heart.

"Diana," it came again, softly, and I approached it with trepidation. "Diana," the bush sighed emotionally, "You came."

I nodded.

The murder bush was psychic; the murder bush was christening me. The garden was packed full of corpses in disarray, mounds of tattered clothing, heaps of flesh and fibres, crowned by huge scarlet blossoms, but the teams of ants and swarms of flies, usually so busy at work, were not to be seen. The garden was dense, the garden was swollen, but the garden was totally still.

The whispering murder bush let out a sudden surge of steaming, stinking milk-white foam, like morning sickness; it splattered me but no more tawdry remains came forth from the plant. There was an absence, I recognized, for me to fill. I had been baptized, given a name and in return, a mission, a quest. I had to contribute a crime to the flourishing greenery that was swallowing up my garden, which would undoubtedly soon swallow the house whole. I accepted.

Inside, I went to my father's bureau. I calmly, decisively, pulled out his ornate revolver with the ivory inlays and waited for him to come back from the petrol station. Being that he was probably wired on crystal, it would take him a long time to run his errand, but I was patient. Finally I heard him come up the drive and through the old screen doors. I noted properly, for the first time since I was a child, the full extent of his Charles and Di Royal Wedding memorabilia collection, lined up ever so nicely on the Welsh Dresser.

"*Bringing Up Baby!*" yelled Myra triumphantly, "It's *Bringing Up Baby* isn't it? Am I right?"

"Yes Myra, you are correct, well done." I smiled.

Father entered the room, saw me with the gun and stopped cold in his tracks. "Ah, baby, my angel, you're not going to shoot your old Dada, are you? You wouldn't hurt your old Pa, would you? I was just playing. You're not gonna shoot me in the balls, letting me bleed to death slowly while you watch, before you turn the gun on yourself and your unborn child are you?"

My father was getting a hard-on.

It was dawn. Outside in the garden the insects had re-sumed their swarming, and the murder bush creaked and groaned as it crept ever closer toward the house. I spent a moment, perusing the hallucinatory tabloid headlines that were wafting into my mind. The unending circus of it all, the frothy, filthy charade enacted by hundreds of salivating perverts who loved nothing more than a murderous little girl and the prospect of a new act of Parliament.

"Oh, how tacky," I thought to myself. "To be slathered across the gutter press and savored as some nympho princess, some sex-slayer from a mid-brow wank fantasy. Gross."

Baby

I disappeared out the window, down an endless dirty path, over broken bones and discarded furniture. Ruins prowled by dirty dogs and defective children; outlawed fascists mumbling to themselves as they dug up skulls, only to rebury them minutes later after kissing them hard, with tongues. Behind me, in the distance, the murder bush groaned. I had not kissed her goodbye, but I knew I had her blessing; even as I slid many kilometers away, I could still hear the cracking of her vines and the moaning of her buds as they burst open and spilt forth new dead.

I was pregnant with my father's daughter; we made our way (the baby and I) regally, over the opalescent tarmac that sparkled with the moon's reflection on leaked oil that seeped from unseen canisters in the shadows. Something snarled, I kicked it.

I spoke to the baby; she was a real, semisolid mass of jelly now. She had eyes, looked like a prehistoric crustacean; she rolled over inside of me, bulbous eyeballs staring out into the darkness. Baby and I exchanged fluids like a pair of old smack heads, best friends, down and out in a church doorway, bumming for change. I poured into her like Holy wine, she flowed into me like my father's semen. A thing of her own making as much as mine, or his. I play music to Baby on a Walkman that I found in a junk shop.

I fasten the headphones around my waist with masking tape, and I play her tape cassettes I bought for 20p each from a garage sale three doors down. They were all unlabeled when we picked them up, but we've listened to them all now and devised our own cataloguing system. A tape marked with a pink dot means classical music, a blue dot means pop music, a yellow dot means weather forecasts or shipping news, and a green dot means recordings of sexual assaults and tortures made in the garage three doors down.

Baby's a snob; she always wants to listen to those tapes marked with pink dots; she says classical music encourages mental development in the fetus. (Baby often talks about herself in the third person). Being a good mother, I play her the music most advantageous for her flourishing faculties; and in return (she being a good daughter), Baby is happy to listen to the tapes with the blue dots when we are taking a shower. Though she maintains an ironic distance, I'm very aware that she's developed a soft spot for *Under Pressure*. We snap our fingers in time to the music; and if Baby's in a real good mood, we duet, with Baby as Freddie Mercury and myself as David Bowie. She has a good heart, really, indulging her old Mum like that; there are a lot of children who wouldn't, you know.

"Baby," I said, "I'm leaving the decision up to you. You're old enough now to take responsibility for yourself. Should we turn left or right when we get to the phone box with all the windows smashed in?"

"Left," said Baby, and went back to sleep.

After a few days on the road, Baby and I became aware that someone was following us. The streets were paved with broken glass and hairpins, inset immaculately and depicting the thirteen labors of Herakles; it was almost beautiful. I told Baby strange tales as we made our way over and under hills, following the back of the Hydra toward the next nearest town—which is to say, truck stop. Baby and I took shelter each night at service stations, sleeping in the bathrooms with the other junkies and the old ladies who wailed the gospel all night long. The electric lights buzzed in and out of consciousness, bathing us occasionally in that blue UV light that makes it impossible (so they say) for you to find your veins and shoot up. I know where all my veins are, thank you very much; I have a guy on the inside feeding me information. Baby counts my veins and logs the flow of traffic like a customs officer; she's so serious.

I can't say it was a particularly pleasant trip, but compared to life back home, life here at least had the attraction of possibility. At home things were forever and endlessly the same; it was always rape, rape, rape, a person needs excitement! On the road things can happen, they do happen. Why, just last weekend, when Baby and I were ripping off a drugstore, we met a fortune-teller who read our palms for free. He made two small incisions in my left hand, and told us that we should prepare ourselves to deal with a tall, dark stranger; and Baby asked, "Do you mean the man who is following us?"

"Exactly," said the fortuneteller. "Now run, because the security guards have you two on tape sticking those bottles of shampoo up your sweater."

It was my sixteenth birthday; I had decided that thirteen didn't fully reflect my capabilities as an artist and a mother, so I grew up very quickly. In the time it took us to walk to the next nearest town (approximately 12 days), I aged three years. My body was an entirely different shape, and I was legally fuckable. Baby, however, was being stubborn; she said that just because I'd gotten ahead of myself didn't mean that she had any intention in rushing to maturation. I didn't mind though; I didn't much relish the idea of pushing her out (especially if it was going to cause me as much pain as it did getting her in there); and to be honest, I'd grown very fond of her and liked having her around the house.

So we lived on in our little truck stop paradise, our little house on the prairie, denim hot pants, bubble gum, slutty lip glosses, Americana rah! rah! rah! In absolutely depraved conditions of bucolic innocence, so naïve and disheveled, but embalmed with the glamour of youth and poverty, our lifestyle was so ragged yet unexpectedly optimistic that we could have been either the poster flower children for Haight Street circa 1971 or the emaciated, toothless leftovers of the decade-long speed jag that came after. Of course we were neither. The references, though intentional, are more metaphorical than literal. We were born so very much later, just as the thread of time snapped for good; and decades like plastic beads on a costume necklace had scattered across the carpet.

Baby had the best sense of humor and was very astute and not at all tyrannical. At the supermarket I'd give her the grocery list, and she'd tot up a running total of everything we picked up, just as though we had any intention of paying for it. Even at bedtime, Baby was always the one to pick out which toilet cubicle we'd sleep in; she had an uncanny spatial understanding. Every evening, we'd scrawl our tag on the bathroom wall: *Diana and Baby were here (Time/Date)*. Baby, I knew, found these to be moments of great historical significance and imagined that when archaeologists unearthed these sites (after the great thunder-and-dust storms of the future) they would catalogue our graffiti as important evidence as to what went wrong in our primitive society. I knew all of this, not because Baby told me (no, she was much too shy to talk about her daydreams); but because many times in those few months we lived in the lavatories she yelled it all out in her sleep.

Sometimes she yelled so loudly that all the other losers and acid heads in the women's room would wake up and start screaming back at us.

"Lady, you better keep your child quiet, or I am going to perform my very own legally patented method of caesarean section on you, right in this here restroom!"

Shoes would come over the top of our stall, thrown alongside bloody panty liners, by irate women trying to sleep away their junk sicknesses. In a cacophony of howls and a hailstorm of bric-a-brac I would wake Baby up and say; "Baby, you are a somniloquist, and you are going to get our asses kicked! You shouldn't eat cheese before bed."

It was on just such a morning that I awoke with a start, amongst the filthy discarded cunt rags and bags of liquefying shredded iceberg lettuce, to hush Baby, and realized the time as I stepped outside into the sunlight.

It was 6:05 AM, a mere two minutes before the lavatory attendant would come in and hose down the bathrooms with her homemade solution of sulfuric acid and honey. Being that the loo lady was as blind as a bat and as merciless as any American President, several of our community had been permanently disfigured by the early morning cleaning procedure, having slept too late and too long. Usually, she started her day with the decalcifying of the men's room, and the screams of tramps as their faces melted off often acted as our alarm clock. However, of late the old devil had started mixing things up, and we never could be sure who would get the hose first. After 6:07 AM, anyone's flesh could be stripped from anyone's bones, without remorse, or for that matter, access to health care.

That was the morning of my seventeenth birthday, when I stepped out of the petrol station bathroom and into the sunlight, shining so brightly that it melted the tarmac beneath my feet. The world was in meltdown, only taking forever to collapse; it refused to give up the ghost and just-fucking-die.

Occasionally, I would take off all my clothes and press myself into the dirt, whispering to the soil, "It's okay, it's all going to be okay. You don't have to be strong anymore, you can just fade out and no one will blame you for it."

But the earth was stubborn and denied it was ill, terminally ill; she just scrawled a little more lipstick wildly across her pock-marked cheeks and said, "See? I'm just fine."

I knew she was crying out for euthanasia, and I knew that to be my task. I heard the murder bush whisper my name.

The name *Diana* came repeatedly in seductive murmurs with gentle determination, on the breeze, confirming my comprehension. That's when I decided to make a mercy killing for planet Earth my mission. I had committed one murder, I could commit more (once you've killed your childhood pet, surely nothing else could be as hard). I took this blessed mission as a nun takes holy orders. The quest descended on me as a mantle from Heaven, the tongue of the Holy Flame; it was the best birthday present ever.

I felt Baby sigh as she pissed inside me.

Two Catholic missionaries, black ladies in God-fearing floral shoe/hat/purse sets, ran up to me singing what I first thought was a spiritual hymn but which I quickly recognized to be *Happy Birthday*. Baby giggled. "Surprise!" and the two old ladies presented me with a sponge cake, garnished with royal icing and, atop it, a random number of candles aflame. I had tears in my eyes as the heat of the day melted the rubber soles of my shoes, gluing them to the pavement.

"Make a wish!" said Baby.

I closed my eyes.

As a special treat, Baby and the two Catholic missionaries had arranged a fireworks display of sorts. We were to walk downtown for the frivolities, to the headquarters of the last remaining Monotony Media outlet, which spanned two blocks. It was, in fact, the only surviving building in the capital (though news bulletins vigorously denied this by showing wide shots of various decaying facades of former residences).

All the way, as the four of us walked, taking turns to carry the cake, we were aware that we were (still) being followed, at a distance of maybe ten meters, by a man in a banana-yellow convertible. He wore a raincoat and maintained an expression of casual, coincidental nonchalance; and all the way to town the Catholic missionaries sang out *We Shall Overcome*, which I thought was very cheerful. Baby, however, was quickly bored (she has a low tolerance for repetition) and insisted on listening to *Carmina Burana* on her Walkman all the way through the desert.

When, eventually, we made it to the outskirts of the capital, she sat bolt upright inside me, sending aqueous shock waves through my body, and started practicing her French lest anyone think her unsophisticated. She kicked herself when she realized that she had left her best blue hat at home; how she would face the other grand society dames she simply did not know.

We spent the morning sipping lemonade and eating the popcorn we bought from a child with a dirty face and a basket of goodies. Taking our pews outside Monotony Media (at a safe distance), we watched the assaults on this last vestige of cultural power. Children strapped with dynamite blew themselves up outside the television studios, setting off car alarms and shattering the windows of studios with talk shows. Little boys and little girls, dressed in their school uniforms, with balaclavas pulled down over their faces, ran toward the building. As soon as the first bullet hit them they detonated themselves, sending out a storm of steel nails into the muscled and suntanned bodies of the former celebrities who now worked as security guards outside the television station.

The children blew themselves up daily, ever more bloodily, ever more cunningly, even being so bold as to walk right up to Superman and ask for his autograph before triggering their explosives. The blood, shit and human mucus dripped from the walls, pooling up in puddles, with little balaclavaed heads bobbing about in them, little organs still twitching, splashing and leaping wildly in the mud. I saw that the blood that spilled spelled out the name of God in Aramaic, or an old advertising slogan from a Coca-Cola commercial. I couldn't quite tell.

Great big groans came from the wounded and the dying, scattered about the automatic doors at the entrance to the studio. Seven Holy Transsexuals, in full mourning dress and wailing louder than any of the blast victims, appeared. They rolled around in the splattered entrails, staining their bright white robes crimson and crawled on their hands and knees, collecting the tiny shoes of the children and the dismembered limbs of the television personalities, as they tore out their own hair and wove all the fragments into a tapestry.

Then off they went to recycle, to sell the usable body parts and the soles of the children's shoes to those who possessed the power to reanimate the dead. There were scientists and sorcerers who could make hybrids from the remains: creatures with the bulging biceps and lacerated torsos of deceased professional wrestlers and the legs of hosiery models, topped with the blond head of a girl of nine, whose face had been blown away by dynamite.

A few of these patched-up Frankensteins were toddling around amongst the explosions and the wailings of the Holy Transsexuals. I found the vision of these zombie sex maniacs slightly arousing (the undead are famed for their unquench-able lust and their dedication to satisfying their lovers), or at least the scene quelled my nausea. Then I noticed that Baby and I were splattered with blood as well, and I felt a violent contraction. The spasm of pain was really quite something, and I thought I must have been going into labor amongst these dead and dying. I realized, however, that it was a false alarm, that Baby was just being a cunt because her tape cas-sette had finished and she wanted me to turn it over. Glancing at the two Catholic missionaries who had watched the vio-lence unfold without comment, I noticed (even, I think, before they had realized it themselves) that their eyeballs had been blown clean through the back of their heads by the force of the explosions. They sat there apparently unaware, with light spilling through the bloody eye sockets of their skulls.

The taller of the pair turned to the shorter and said, "Mercy! I don't feel so good this afternoon. I just don't feel quite myself."

"No, Charity," replied the shorter of the pair, "you don't look it."

Love Is a Stranger in an Open Car

With the banana-yellow convertible still trailing us at an ever-greater distance, Baby and I, and the two Catholic missionaries left the capital on foot. Usually the capital is where the narrative experiences one of its climaxes, but not for us. In times such as ours, the only hope was to get to the suburbs and sit down in front of MTV, to find that Pepsi-commercial normality that we'd read about so often in those tattered sheets of the *New York Times* that now served as window panes in the shanty houses of Great Britain. Thus, we were on the road again to chocolate-box homes set on immaculate, unnaturally green lawns, to anonymous perfection.

Partway through the jungle (don't ask me girl, I didn't put it there) we came across a twenty-four-hour diner. So as not to frighten the other patrons, the missionaries put on heart-shaped sunglasses and followed Baby and me inside. We all ordered pancakes. Baby dressed her pancakes in butter and maple syrup, I dressed mine in jam because I'm British, and the missionaries dressed theirs with great big cold dollops of ice cream.

"Oh, you wannit à la mode, which means with ice cream?" said the waitress.

Our pancakes were each exactly one-and-a-half inches

29

thick, they were light, they were moist, and they looked so tasty that Baby and I could almost imagine staying at the diner, working a couple shifts, and maybe picking up a trucker sweetheart on the side. (Baby is such a romantic!) I sniffled, and I wished that I hadn't killed Sisterhood; she would have made such a lovely truck-stop playmate for Baby, and she could probably have taken a job in our daydream diner, washing dishes or peeling potatoes. "Oh well, that's life, kid!" I said to myself under my breath.

The missionaries insisted that we say grace before we ate. Baby and I were more than happy to oblige; in fact, Baby said grace aloud.

"Jam pots, lamp posts, scapegoats, Holy ghosts, remote controls, and Joan of Arc be with us as we devour the flesh of this most sacred vittles, and thee unto thee unto she and yee, beseech thine only daughter to come fuck with me when the sun goes down."

"Amen," said the missionaries in unison, a little tear forming in what was formerly their eyes. (Baby is a powerful orator.)

In the diner, which was frankly inoffensive, a plainly unremarkable sort of place, I noticed, a lot of people had clocks for faces, all set at different times; it was the fashion in that part of the world. I found it very becoming, but Baby looked down her nose at it, saying that the fashionable people can never be stylish; and the missionaries took it for a sure sign of the Apocalypse and crossed themselves over and over, throwing handfuls of NutraSweet over their shoulders. The Apocalypse indeed. I'd been waiting around for a decade and a half for the Apocalypse, and she was still a no-show. I'd been stood up by the end of the world (which I thought was typifuckingcal), and so I had to take things into my own hands, only I didn't yet quite know how.

Baby ate her pancakes too quickly and got hiccups.

The sun was coming up or going down; from our window we could see the horizon turn the color synthetic American cheese does when it melts on a grilled cheddar sandwich in a cast-iron frying pan. The jungle all around us took on a painterly quality, and I half expected one of Rousseau's stupefied tigers to come hurtling out of the weeds and bushes.

In their day, before they were married, the Catholic missionaries—who were born in Croydon—had been sent on a mission to Africa in general, where they had preached to the unconverted jungle cats. I suppose the smell of the wet foliage outside the diner triggered a memory for them, because they began to reminisce about those days. Their booming crystal voices and the might with which they expressed the love of Christ all over the continent caused many wild animals (and several domesticated ones, too) to desist in their heathen ways and convert to the true faith. Pretty soon Mercy and Charity had one of the largest and most vibrant parishes in all of Christendom, although it was made up exclusively of indigenous animals; and the Archbishop of Westminster could not have been more pleased. Their church become so famous that people from all over Africa would flock every Sunday to see the tigers and lions incant their acts of contrition and roar along with Psalms 111 and 112, as well as 113—a particular favorite with the leopardesses.

Jungle cats were, it must be said, quite a sight in their Sunday best, manes combed down demurely in favor of delicate little pillbox hats, the jaguars with rosary beads, and panthers with pressed skirt suits. Local, then national, then international media heard the sensational story of wild beasts tamed by God's love and made this divine spiritual mystery into a tacky teatime tale. The congregation was disgusted. Seeing themselves double-crossed and exposed, made into celebrities by gossip magazines, the animals revolted and mauled to death every last journalist, and every gawping church goer, sparing only Mercy and Charity for love. The ladies were promptly removed from their beloved post and sent on a new mission, to minister to the forlorn and insane at international gas stations.

My attention drifted back to the purple aura radiating from the stack of now soggy pancakes in front of me. It was about this time that I realized that there was a white fellow sitting next to me, right at my elbow, at our table in this twenty-four hour diner. Our shiny red vinyl booth had hardly squeaked at his arrival, and I had been so caught up in the reminiscences of the missionaries that I hadn't even noticed him arrive. Scratch that. Explain nothing. He was there, and it didn't matter how. (If you go about looking for sense, asking for logic, and putting your faith in reason, then you are asking for trouble and you will deserve it when two big thugs named Senseless Violence and Why God Why? drag you down an alley and beat you up).

"So," said Baby, always quickly off the mark, "you're the one who's been following behind us in the car? How come you've stopped? Outta gas?" Baby always fancied herself as a kind of Humphrey Bogart private eye in these kinds of situations.

"Nothing of the sort, well, yes, actually, well, do you ladies want to go for a spin? Breakfast is on me, of course."

The missionaries blushed. It was a long time since they'd been asked out on a date.

"What's the big idea, wise guy?" asked Baby.

"Oh nothing, nothing of the sort. It's just that well, yes, actually, my horoscope said that I was going to find you here and that you were my only, only hope. You see, I am the son and heir of nothing in particular, and unless I find my poor old mother, I'll be disinherited, and then I shan't be able to pay her medical bills. She keeps insisting on having glass jaws fitted, even though I've told her that for a champion skier it is simply a terrible idea. "

"You're Thackeray Clinton, aren't you? I've read all about you," said the waitress, filling his cup with coffee from a vase of flowers, "You're the son of that international woman of mystery, aren't you, what's her name? The spy, the actress, or whatever she is. And you've been married three times already, each time to a more fabulously wealthy faggot." She pulled out one succulent breast and lactated lovingly into his coffee cup.

"Sugar?"

He shook his head.

"You've made an art of marrying well," the waitress continued.

"Well, not quite an art darling," he replied drolly, "more

of a craft."

Baby, who's a soft touch for a sob story, said, "All in favor of hitting the road with this scurvy seadog say 'Aye.'"

Unanimously, everybody in the diner said, "Aye." Every
clock face, the deaf cook, the waitress who was a cyborg, and,
pulled by cosmic magnetism, myself. We had a deal. He put
down a fifty-drachma note and we left, under a shower of
confetti people made on the spot from freshly torn pieces of
toast.

"Don't forget to write!" shouted the waitress who was a
cyborg. Then she short-circuited fatally and was put to work
as a fridge freezer.

Upon departing the diner we boarded the famed banana
yellow convertible. Baby and I sat in the front seat next to our
new friend, and the Catholic missionaries sat stashed in the
back with their trunks, fittingly enough. The banana-yellow
convertible was lined inside with pistachio-green lizard skin.
The color of it made me long for California. I had half a mind
right there and then to blow a chunk of Baby's college fund
on a one-way ticket to San Jose just so I could fall in love with
avocado all over again. Monterey Bay, the asparagus capital
of the world. Gilroy, the home of garlic. Produce, produce,
produce! We fastened our seatbelts.

"Remind me to tell you some snowy night about the
time I looked into the heart of an artichoke," our new friend
said, and we all nodded, feigning interest. "I am a millionaire
speed freak and a nihilist. Name your destination, ladies."

Baby groaned. "Oh how original! Just our luck to be
landed with someone like *him* as a chauffeur, this whole epi-

sode is a little too Nan Goldin for me."

"Girl, we are giving full on *Ballad of Sexual Dependency* realness in this car tonight!" Charity and Mercy were staring deep into each other's eye sockets and trying on each other's wigs. It was the sexiest thing I had seen in quite some time, and I had to fight very hard to keep from getting a hard on, lest I make Baby feel uncomfortable.

Thackeray changed the subject; "So, why do you call her Baby?"

"Because, I'm her mother and she's my baby," I replied. "Do you think we could go via Hearst Castle? Only I've been dying to go there for the longest time."

"Oh, absolutely," said Thackeray. "We can go via the castle, we'll just take Highway 1 up the coast! But, say, where is it we're trying to end up?"

"We'll tell you when we get there," said Baby. "Now drive."

Fore!

The wind was in our hair as we roared toward certain victory, down the freeway motorway autobahn autoroutes, those entangled strands of spaghetti that now encircled the entire globe. The wind was in our hair, toxic and noxious, and on occasions actually singeing our French plaits, our cornrows, and our beehives, melting our extensions to the sides of our faces like dime store dishware in a death camp oven. In the abrasive air, our hair became celluloid, transparent and syrupy, rolling down our cheeks like hot fudge sauce, into our eyes and our mouths. To keep it from pouring off our scalps entirely, we pulled silk scarves over our heads, as we continued along the coastal road, staring over the cliff's edge at our own craggy deaths, with the greedy Pacific longing for our sundried bones. The headscarves covered up our bald patches like Elizabeth Taylor's fondest memories of herself, and fluttered ragged in the wind, like schizoid consciences, like the battle colors of Elizabeth the First's victorious fleet in Cadiz, as they slaughtered the Spanish Catholics and took back marvelous jewels to enrich the already miraculous wealth of their monarch.

Thackeray was swerving all over the road, which could have been a problem had anyone else been driving on the highway. But as it was empty, since no one else could afford fossil fuels, he was only a hazard to himself. And us, of course.

"Are you high?" asked Baby, shaken from her nap by the screeching of the convertible's breaks. "Have you been drinking?"

"Only every second of my life!" said Thackeray. "But that hardly matters. The fact is, I can't actually drive."

The poor boy was a prisoner really—well, not really, but metaphorically. His mother, Myra, was a prisoner really, and not metaphorically, but literally. She had been banged up in a rather grand Tudor mansion, sometime after the revolution, a hostage at the hands of any number of terrorist cells depending on which tabloid you read. She had been a pin-up sex bomb glamour girl of the ancient régime, and her disappearance had never since been out of the news, ever since the day she was snatched out of the arms of her lover Charles de Gaulle whilst opening a supermarket.

People speculated that de Gaulle was tired of Myra and had had her kidnapped, to free up some time for a romance with the transsexual temptress Lola Lasagne, or that he perhaps staged the whole thing as a publicity stunt to help sales of his fragrance *Eau de Fame*. Then there were those who proposed Myra had been spirited away by the legendary underage freedom fighters The Valeries as part of their campaign to obliterate patriarchal oppression and parking fines, whilst others said it was clearly the work of the Sheryl Crow fan club. Others speculated that Myra had staged the whole thing on the advice of Greta Garbo, who was of the opinion that she ought to disappear behind a veil of glamorous tittle-tattle, before she lost her looks. Some suggested that the plot was hatched by a cabal of Myra's former lovers, amongst them JFK, Simon Bolivar, and Queen Sofia of Spain (Myra only dated people with airports named after them), who had disappeared her for their own nefarious eroticisms. Who knows? Gosh, it's just all so exciting!

All anyone could say for sure was that Myra was there at one point, and then quite simply, she was gone. Thackeray was three at the time of her kidnapping and had not taken it well. Though he came into the ten-million-dollar insurance inheritance before he left kindergarten, nothing could take the place of old Mommy Dearest in his poor little heart. Admittedly, she had been an absentee parent, too busy seducing the yacht-owning heads of government and smuggling blueprints in her stockings to do any real parenting, but Thackeray was a smart kid and managed to romanticize her quite successfully in her absence. He told me once (when we made love in a hot tub in Albuquerque) that if it hadn't been for the outrageously glamorous, highly publicized, raucously reported, frothily fraudulent kidnapping of his mother, he probably would never have become a narcotics fiend and an international playboy, which really would have been a shame.

Who would have driven us onward to nowhere then? Endlessly tearing up the highways, forever in pursuit of the opposite direction of his mother's many possible outcomes. Of course, he didn't really want to find her, didn't care a jot for that particular narrative. He was happy to be motivated, in a manner abstractly flavored with emotional sensations, by the turning of the wheels under the Tudor mansion in which she was imprisoned, as it rolled onward from one caravan park to the next, drawing him magnetically like a somnambulist in its wake. Where she went he would follow, as the water follows the moon, unhappily.

Against such a high-octane plot, I felt just like a movie star sitting beside Thackeray and yelping as we tore down that winding road through the Hollywood Hills, tires spinning, grasping for traction, panic stricken, gasping for breath. The car roared on almost of its own volition. We were passengers, we were porcelain, and we were headed we did not know where. I could have been Grace Kelly. I could have been Jayne Mansfield, James Dean, Isadora Duncan, Helmut Newton, or Bessie Smith, and no one would have noticed. I could have been.

I noticed that if I quickly wound the hands on Thackeray's speedometer with my fingertips, though the car itself would obviously go no faster, the scenery we passed would slip by at a much quicker pace. The world rolled by on command, every rule of logic lost, and in its place, revelations on relativity we could not hope to comprehend. If I could now lay out a new location like a fresh roll of linoleum, I wondered, who had been calling the shots previously and why had he insisted on spatial fixity? After all these years, the leasehold on geography was finally up; and whereas the world was once flat, and later spherical, it was now reminiscent of the whirling insides of a food processor, hurling the contents together in a fatal centrifugal waltz.

"Life is entirely pasteboard!" I cried out, full of nonchalant terror, while locations flashed past my eyes as though I were watching a spasmodic television set flick through hundreds of channels at once.

The Catholic missionaries roared with laughter as the foliage became a warm green breeze, a luscious Impressionist's soundscape of blaring foghorns, church bells and groans from a Wurlitzer; they said the sensation reminded them of their days in Africa and they wept for the loss of their eyeballs.

I took my finger off the speedometer, and another new location began to crystallize around us. Somewhere European, with bomb craters, history, expanses of forest. No, there was no sunroof in the banana-yellow convertible, but I stood up on my seat anyway and pulled down my shirt to show everyone my swollen, milky teen tits. As I mentioned, however, there was no one else on the autobahn. I was exposing myself to no one, though I would have taken a picture on my disposable camera; but Baby had insisted we pull over to visit the zoo, and I had long run out of exposures.

Charlie

It was night, inevitably, and Thackeray was asleep at the wheel. The car continued on steadily, down the bullet-straight autobahn, in almost total silence, with just a hint of a purr— good kitty. Baby was asleep inside me, she was as big as a football now, had congealed, hardened into a small human. She was fully baked, and I was nineteen. She snored softly, tooting like a toy trumpet every minute or so, her tiny body floating around in years of recycled shit. For once she wasn't talking in her sleep.

In the back of the car, the missionaries (wearing matching pajamas, of course) slept wrapped around each other like a pair of pythons intent on murder, and no noise came from them. The radio, barely even audible, played Noel Coward (that's what they play on radio stations in Berlin), and the world turned black and white. It was post-war Europe, dark outside the car, the sky little troubled by stars, nothing stirred. We cruised on indefinitely, ate the road like licorice, pulled ourselves along by our teeth, and it hurt. Quite clearly I heard the voice of the murder bush hanging on the silent, desolate breeze, rasping and heaving, lusty as ever, as though the sounds had been cut out of the night air with great precision using an X-acto knife. I heard the murder bush wrap her tendrils around my father, snap him like a twig, and swallow him whole. "Diana," gasped the murder bush, "Di-a-na," long and low.

Then there was silence.

From out of nowhere came a monstrously large snail, a hulking, mammoth thing, creeping slowly across the highway, bisecting the road with its slow and oozy trails. The snail turned its gigantic head to look at me, the tentacles standing erect in alarm. Then, perhaps relieved that we were not a pack of poachers, raised its sluggish body a little and displayed a great goofy smile on its sopping mouth, dragging its preposterous weight out of the convertible's trajectory. The snail pulled itself parallel with the car and slithered alongside us for a few kilometers, looking at me and giggling to itself occasionally. Each chuckle grew louder and louder, until I was simply forced (by politeness if nothing else) to ask, "What's so funny?"

"Well," said the snail with a laugh, "I know something you don't know."

"And?" I retorted. "So do most people. My formal education was rather rudimentary."

"Did you ever study…" and here the snail broke off with a snigger. "Did you ever study human *biology*?"

"Not in any depth," I replied. "Sisterhood, my dog, was doing an online course in applied physiognomy, and occasionally I would read over her shoulder, but I don't think that counts."

"Ha! It's too funny!" guffawed the snail.

I rolled my eyes.

"Snails!" it continued, by now almost beside itself with mirth. "Snails! Have a penis *and* a vagina!" It roared with such convulsed hysteria that the road actually started to shake and I feared for our safety, and yet everyone else slept on.

"Is that supposed to be a joke?" I asked in earnestness.

"It's the truth," chuckled the snail, "but nature's jokes are always the worst!"

The snail exploded with snickers, bellowing great big chuckles, almost aggressively, almost beginning to hyperventilate. In this state of distended hilarity the snail heaved itself around in a ludicrously inelegant about-face and slithered off in the opposite direction, repeatedly snorting, "Is it a joke?" to itself.

The car and I paid the snail no mind, and we sailed on inevitably as though the road were a conveyor belt, the world a Model T factory, and the future a windshield wiper to be added before we rolled out into the big, bright, white world. Great, hulking skeletons lined the way, the bones of long dead dinosaurs, yearning for love, sculptural under moonbeams. (Moonbeams? What the hell is a moonbeam? Light is light.) Enormous thigh bones, femurs, ribcages, skulls, boners, all so massive, dwarfing me and my banana-yellow convertible, a handful of hours from Paris. As we rattled by, I brushed my outstretched hands against these calcified outcroppings, my fingertips kissed them gently, and I think I fell in love.

A flickering speck on the horizon caught my eye, but in the darkness, I could not comprehend it. My eyes could not reveal to my mind exactly what it was waiting for me there up ahead. I groaned, more from exhaustion, than from anxiety; in spite of the insanity and the depravity of the sociopathic junk-yard to which the world had been reduced, I was not afraid. I did not fear that this emerging expression of motion would actually show itself to be my executioner. Even as we neared the mysteriously moving thing, I felt no need to steel myself for another nightmare, no need to brace myself; no, I could hear the murder bush whisper my name in an orgasmic build up, so I did not feel scared. Instead I felt a bottomless curiosity.

"What is it," I whispered, careful not to wake Baby, "that flickers like that, out here at the end of the earth?"

I hit the headlights. They were startlingly bright, like spotlights, turning the desert into the moon, and they threw out magnificent columns of light. Quite casually, Charlie Chaplin, sparkling with cinematic luminosity, was revealed leaning on a lamppost at the corner of the street. As he stood there in his funny little hat, the car passed him, and he barely noticed, until I turned off the engine and we rolled to a slow stop. At this point, Charlie Chaplin (holding a sign that read, "Anywhere but here!") snapped into action and tramped toward the convertible—I nearly wept like Mary Magdalene over Christ's feet.

Stepping out of the car barefoot into the still warm sand, I was careful to look for snakes. I recognized then that the sand *was* snakes, a thick, blistered carpet of androgynous snakes fucking and killing beneath my footsteps. I made my way to Charlie Chaplin, who had stopped just an arm's length behind the car and stood there mournfully with his sign and his suitcase, looking like a wax replica of Charlie Chaplin put outside a roadside souvenir stand to attract children.

I asked him, "Do you sell souvenirs?"

"No, I never want to come here again." He spoke only in dialogue cards, which he held up in front of him, then dropped to the ground to be swallowed by snakes when he reached the end of his sentence. "I've seen all of your movies!" he continued.

I blushed, fancy Charlie Chaplin being a fan of mine! I gestured that he should come closer but he looked at the convertible and asked, "Why are you driving around with a car full of corpses?"

"They're not dead," I assured him, "just sleeping."

In the future, Charlie Chaplin and I would stop late at night deep into the road trip, and fuck. Whilst everyone else was asleep, we'd sneak out of the car and go roll about in the dirt, with the snakes pouring over us and into us, at every opportunity. Short men tend to have outrageously big dicks. Charlie Chaplin would look at me with those incredible eyes of his; he'd somersault backward, trip over his suitcase, and rip open his pants until I couldn't control my desire for him a moment longer. In the future Charlie Chaplin and I would watch countless dawns in the desert and feed each other wild berries, painting each other's lips with them, slipping them slowly into each other's assholes somewhere deep into Bavaria, just outside Munich. In the future Charlie Chaplin would put his moustache between my legs and knicker lace and make me lose control, and in the future Charlie Chaplin would give me an emerald necklace, and in the future Charlie Chaplin would write our names in the sand as the sea washed in, and in the future I would be the future Mrs. Charles Chaplin and Baby would officiate the wedding. But for now, I offered Charlie Chaplin a ride and he accepted, sliding in alongside the Catholic missionaries, silently.

I turned the keys in the engine and the car started up again, manifest destiny gliding onward into the inky night of new situations. I killed the headlights. I turned off the radio; the stars on their dimmer switch went out, and the sun, oversleeping, did not rise. In absolute darkness and absolute quiet we went—I think I fell asleep too—but in those circumstances it would be hard to tell.

For a little while we traveled on as ice skaters are wont to do across endless glassy lakes, cold cold cold as only the desert at night can be; and I felt Charlie Chaplin's hand reach for my shoulder and his emotions bleed all over me, pour down my chest, saturate my gown, pool at my feet.

"You know Charlie," I said, "we're a lot alike."

Charlie Chaplin was the biggest star in the world, the only man more famous than him was Hitler; and girl, face it, that bitch mopped the look. The moustache, the parting in the hair, the touch of kohl, that maniacal glint in the eye, please. Guilty as charged. Charlie Chaplin invented celebrities. Charlie Chaplin invented fame. Charlie Chaplin invented money and success and critical reception. Before him there was nothing but poets starving to death in their garrets and actresses rotting from need of material and artists choking on their paintbrushes, so badly repressed was their lust. Before him culture was a sandstorm, a drought, and he was a raindrop moistening the cracked skin of the world, a teardrop from

Christ's own eye.

"We're both exiles, Charlie," I whispered.

I had already fallen in love with him. He was a homeless punk like me, a wandering Jew—discontinuations, excommunications, the end of a line that has no end; purgatory, even, had closed its doors to us. All we had was the nothingness around us, the giant lizard of a pitch-black night flicking its gruesome tongue somewhere ahead, *nox infinita*. Maybe we were a car full of corpses, I don't know.

Then!

We hit a ditch, or a dip in the road, or a stone, or an animal, or the edge of a cliff, or the Eiffel Tower, or a Doris Day record, or five o'clock in the afternoon. We collided with something, and it sent us spinning. A Victorian tea set shattered, cupboard doors flew open, maids fell to their knees in prayer, and the grandfather clock split right down the middle. Our car overturned midair, we were bound for a bad end, we rode a rollercoaster loop-the-loop, we hadn't bought a ticket, bolts on the wooden structure came loose, and we all screamed awake and hit the ground. Golden coins showered us, shattering our windscreen and waking up the dog, fracturing bones severely in some cases, spraining ankles, tearing ligaments, setting off the car alarm like suicide bombers in Baghdad during the last war—no the one before that, no the one before that, no the one before that. We were spilt like a deck of cards drunkenly dealt at a séance and scattered across the vinyl floor of a discount kitchen supply store. Dazed. Cartoon budgerigars tweeting in circles above our heads. Next! Next! Next! Move along, there's nothing to see here.

The sun rose and poured in through the empty eye sockets of the missionaries (their sunglasses misplaced in the commotion of the car wreck) illuminating the scene for us. Thackeray turned to look behind him, found himself behind everyone, searched his pocket for a light, remembered not to smoke near Baby so stuck his hands in his pants instead. Lying, sprawled awkwardly, pieces of a jigsaw puzzle rammed into the wrong picture, Baby and I and Charlie Chaplin and the Catholic missionaries were encircled by Thackeray's dewy dawn footsteps.

"I have the worst hangover," he said. "Really, the *worst*."

He coughed, holding his balls. No one responded to him. Somewhere not too far away, or maybe so far away we were only hearing the echo of its death, an egg was frying sunny side up. (I've always been suspicious of eggs. What if someone were to decide to split me open like a roe and harvest me? It *could* happen).

"And what makes it worse," Thackeray continued, "is that I am seemingly pointless. Does anyone know? Can anyone tell me what my dramatic function in this narrative is? Something to do with my mother, I suppose."

"Just be grateful you have an opposable name," Mercy grumbled like Frankenstein's monster.

"Dr. Frankenstein's monster to you," said Charity.

Charlie Chaplin produced a dialogue card that simply read, "EXACTLY!"

Baby is such a late sleeper. She practically missed the whole thing (she'd been up late reading *Vile Bodies* so I forgave her). Coming into consciousness, as one late to breakfast arrives in the kitchen just in time to catch the tail end of the conversation, Baby took in a casual scan of the scene as she would have plucked a slice of toast from the toast rack, and felt the atmosphere. Choosing not to speak until she had a clearer idea of the situation (Baby's so pragmatic!), she attended to her silk dressing gown, making sure her ample pin-up cleavage wasn't too exposed, but obviously not too disguised either. A woman has to work her assets, doesn't she? Los Angeles Los Angeles Los Angeles. Baby saw that she'd walked in on something nasty and chose, honorably, to do something about it. With a bow in her hair and her best doped-up Shirley Temple intonation she gasped, "Gee Mister! Say, aren't you Charlie Chaplin?"

Christmas Day 1943

Reassembled. We tore through the desert and into Berlin, somehow an oasis in the sand, or a mirage, yeah, maybe an illusion in the dunes. I listened to the radio, mainly white noise, fuzz, out of which came a mellow voice reading the news, or the story my life. I recognized the voice from somewhere, but where? The movies? A daydream? My mother, perhaps? No, it was the murder bush, now broadcasting on FM radio:

> *Hello, Beat Boppers. You are listening to the Federal Republic's nonstop hit music station, Tropicalia FM, with you awl through the night. Diana, riding shotgun through Germany, with her NBFs, as the children say, is feeling under pressure from so many directions. She's been in that damn banana-yellow convertible since time began, almost, and it seems that the road is no closer to ending. Just a few hours ago the whole company stopped to smash a piñata outside Frankfurt and stumbled upon three outrageously rich women, models, the wives of C.E.Os who went into exile after the crash and left all their cash in Swedish bank accounts. These women, dressed to-the-nines in cocktail dresses tack-stitched to their bodies by the reanimated corpse of Cristóbal Balenciaga himself (at*

a premium of course) and decorated in enough baubles to make the Queen of Sheba throw a fit, sat around a picnic table and pounded the woodchip surface with their gloved hands, banging out the rhythm of L'Internationale. They propounded the saving graces of Communism as the only way to save the world from what it had become, and they ordered more martinis. Hello, Worker!

I changed the channel, tripped the station. I felt awkward; hearing about myself from the exterior exerted a pressure on me, so I turned the radio off definitively. I became aware that Thackeray had been telling a story. I was relieved because it meant that nobody had paid any attention to the murder bush's radio ramblings. (Thackeray is no Baby but he is a very capable public speaker.)

"My first wife Freya was a goddess, but I myself am only a princess, so it was doomed from the start. When I say goddess, I do mean *goddess*. I don't mean fashion model. I don't mean she had her own cable TV show or advertised shampoo in women's magazines. I mean *goddess*, as in 'immortal being,' the Goddess of sex and warfare, in fact, though her franchise only operated in Northern Europe, outside of which she was considered with the same vague contempt as most Australian actresses.

Sex and warfare is an interesting combination, though we never fucked; nor did we for that matter go to war. We had other pastimes. For example, parties. We were club kids and spent all our time, and all our parent's monies, dressing up and messing up. In the 1920s she was the first woman to ditch

51

her corset in favor of a boxy little flapper dress all fringed in French beading, and she stuck an enormous peacock feather in her hair to boot. We roared around the hotspots of interwar Europe on credit, telling everyone who'd listen that we were Ernest and Pauline Hemmingway and running up magnificent tabs in their name. Why, I think we might have even written *The Sun Also Rises,* but I couldn't be sure; there was a lot of bad ketamine going around at that time, and a person could become quite convinced of anything where that was involved.

In the sixties we fell in with Princess Margaret's circle, Snowdon and all that; only Freya never took to Margaret all that well. They had some sort of falling out. We lived it up with Michael Alig in the nineties too, in New York, and Lord knows how we survived *that*! But we did and I've got the pictures to prove it, somewhere, the three of us all painted blue, wearing nothing but tennis shoes and Christmas decorations, shopping at the Rite-Aid on 3rd and 9th.

Freya was the only one who could keep up with me—such an artistic, excitable woman. She could hold her drugs, and she always picked up the tab; you could tell she came from a good family. I came home after a three-day speed jag and found her standing over the remains of a $250,000 ruby necklace with a hammer in her hands, her pupils wildly dilated. I asked her why she had smashed a quarter of a million dollars worth of jewelry to pieces in the middle of a dust bowl Depression. She whimpered and said, 'I thought it was a snake.'

One day she walked out on me. She left a hole in my life that I've never been able to fully fill, try as I might. You know, the last time I was in Los Angeles I booked into Chateau Chateau and called everyone in the yellow pages listed under P for Penis and got them to come over to my room and fuck me. Even that didn't suffice; I was full of blood and cum, but I was still empty. And you know, I've been looking for her ever since. Driving up and down these highways like Sisyphus with that rock. "

"Maybe you should just kill yourself," said Charity, the taller of the two Catholic missionaries. "It'd be so much more time efficient, and you would save such a lot on gas."

We drove on.

I wondered if Thackeray was still high now. Probably, what else was he going to do? For a moment, something approximating reality flashed before my eyes. I couldn't tell whether it seemed attractive to me or not, but I recognized it as being preferable to the probable likelihood of spending twenty-five years drifting aimlessly down the motorway in this very car. I decided that at the next petrol station I was going to get out and go it alone, with Baby. I hadn't reckoned on Baby being of a different mind to me; and when I told her about my plan, she flew into a rage.

"These people are our friends now—no, they're our family—and we're in it for life," she declared rather dramatically at the back of an ESSO service station.

"We can't very well stay in that car for the rest of our lives, hurtling down the autoroutes with no direction home, Baby," I said. "Be serious. Mommy loves you."

Baby didn't reply. The tape in her Walkman came to a halt with a very pointed *click*. I realized that she was in love with Thackeray, the way all little girls are in love with faggots, the way I loved Charlie Chaplin.

"You can walk out, just like Thackeray's mother, just like his wife, that's all you know how to do, but I am staying!" she said (Baby watched too many soap operas). "I don't care if we do travel the length and breadth of the universe from now until Armageddon. What else is there to do anyway?"

"I guess you're right," I said reluctantly, and we climbed back into the car.

Baby would never know that everything I had done I had done for her. Baby would never be able to merge that narrative in her head with the narrative she had given me, of boundless selfishness. To her they could only run parallel. Baby was not an idiot, but she was a human, and she needed to be the hero of her own life. She needed me to be an irresponsible slut, and so I was. I vowed I would never disappoint her. It was too painful for her to see the horror I carried like a cross. She did not want to feel responsible for that, though she was born out of it. She needed me to be an outcast in the gutter far from Heaven, so that I might still be saved; but I was not. I was just a woman and barely that.

I had run to save us, had killed and scratched, tricked and slandered, fought and groveled; and I was not sorry, only tinged with a remorse at knowing that Baby could never acknowledge this, that it would blow her apart to face it. She had erected a false consciousness that figured me as the perpetrator of all the wickedness in the world, as a woman who deserved the horrors that had assailed her. To look the reality of her conception in the eye would reduce her to a thick pulp quicker than the abortionist's whirring blades could ever hope to. Nobody can handle a truth so heavy; surely it would stop her heart to hear it. I was now a slave to Baby and her fabrications. I was bound to her, and every atrocity (which I would undoubtedly commit) would tighten those manacles; distance would only make it more excruciating.

A couple of hours later, as the car finally came to an inexplicable standstill in the middle of a blizzard, I gave birth.

The ground was thick with snow, deep snow, tons of cocaine and powdered sugar spilled all across the roads. Pine trees bursting down the hillside on either side of the ravine released cedarn odors into the Mitteleuropa afternoon sky, which was bright blue, the color of revelations. Daydreams melted on my tongue, fake snowflakes coming from the upper level of the theater to pour down on us like a showy finish in a feel-good Christmas play. It was no new ice age—it was ballet—and the snow fell for hours and hours, deep and crisp and even, like justice, mounting as high as the mid-point of the car's wheels before any of us noticed the danger: the danger of being midway through Germany in an open-top convertible as the temperature dropped below freezing and wolves came out of hibernation.

They had slept through a summer, which had made them skinny and lusty and licking at the air for a scent of blood. Traces of blood were leaking out from between my legs, crimson droplets, thick red wine on the pistachio green leather of the banana-yellow convertible. We heard howls.

The Catholic missionaries sat with their sunglasses on, as the snow piled up on their knees in the backseat of the car. Charlie Chaplin said there was nothing for it and set out across the tundra alone, said he'd rather die of hypothermia than wait to be devoured by scavengers. I gasped. Thackeray knocked back a hip flask full of whiskey and stood up on his seat to piss into the snow, carving his name into the frothy mounds with the contents of his overfull bladder. I myself didn't care much if we died from exposure or were ripped limb from limb. I didn't even bother to contemplate what my choice would be if forced by a malicious God to make it. The moon rose alongside the sun and it was mid-winter and time stood still and Baby chose that moment to come into the world; or rather, to come out.

In labor I made more noise than the wolves. I gave birth in a snow bank. I had no medication besides the little whiskey residue I sucked out of Thackeray, which only did a very little to help. I started to believe I was the Virgin lying there in the snow, with the Catholic missionaries ripping up bed sheets (the Devil makes work for idle hands, you see) and belting out *What a Friend We Have in Jesus* over and over through the nine hours of my labor. My blood soaked the snow, and later we would make popsicles from it; but for now I groaned and exhaled and thrashed about with the cold at my back, and screamed for Charlie Chaplin, who didn't come running back to soothe my fevered brow.

Eventually, a throng of wolves hurtled down the hill to attend me in my hour of need. I can't be sure, but I think I saw Sisterhood at the head of the pack, leading them to my aid, her big, fat pink tongue lolling out of her mouth as she ran ahead of the pack, her blond fur demarcating her from the wolves in their silver finery. No, I can't be sure; I was wracked and hysterical with pain, delirious and cold, afraid and willing to believe in anything, just to have something to cling to. Nobody is an atheist on the battlefield.

Thackeray, coming down hard, imagined the wolves were the devil's angels and in turn screamed hysterically, louder even than myself. The missionaries took the shredded bed sheets and tied strips to the pine trees to make a more festive scene, whilst Thackeray began to convulse. I made a snow angel in all my thrashings on the ground. The wolves licked my face, helped me breathe, licked my breasts, took my pulse, licked my cunt, held my hand, licked Baby's face as she burst out. They faxed my doctor back home to tell him that my giving birth had been successful, and even attended to the insurance paperwork.

Upon Baby's full and gracious exit from my body, the wolves gathered around her, circled her and flexed their jaws. I wondered if they would really eat her or if they were just pantomiming. At that moment, Mercy came bounding over with paper hats for everyone to wear and a tray full of prawn mayonnaise vol-au-vents. Charity carried a gramophone, which she wound up and loaded with an LP of Al Jolson singing the hits from *The Jazz Singer*. What a party it was! Boom! I was a woman and an artist and a mother at the age of twenty-one, yet still an ingénue. Baby had been born, I scooped her up out of the slime and the snow, she was quiet and lukewarm, and she looked like a baby. I dressed her in a big yellow sunbonnet and a lime green romper suit that declared, "Grandpa's little angel!"

I put her down in the front seat of the car next to a Thackeray in spasms; he was crashing so badly in the cold that his whole face had turned gray. I left her there and went to follow Charlie Chaplin across the snow on foot, trailing chunks of burgundy placenta behind me every few steps, hoping to catch up with him and bring him back home. The wolves and the missionaries continued to waltz cheek-to-cheek to the gramophone records; they didn't even notice me leave.

I threw off my shoes and followed my man across the white icing-sugar desert. A great big romantic string section started to play, and I ran on. I was Dietrich, he was Gary Cooper, this was Morocco.

But soon enough I admitted that he was gone.

I came to a cliff, sheer rock ten-stories tall, insurmountable, where Charlie Chaplin's footprints stopped. As though he had walked right into the mountain, permeated its skin and found his way deep into its intestines, clambering through the mucus and tubings and the slate-gray inner workings of the cliff, and made a little hollow for himself inside. I pressed my ears against the stone, and I whispered to the rock, hummed little secrets into the cracks and poured out my heart's daydreams against the unfeeling crag, which chose to take no notice of me either way. I asked the mountain, "Won't you let me in? Can't you give shelter to a poor lost soul?"

The rock replied campily but with very little interest, "No dear, I can't! And now let that be the end of it."

So I continued on around the cliff, engaged the snow and ignored the ice, pulled up my socks and walked on. Everything was white. I could barely see a meter ahead of me.

I was lost to the nothingness. Backward was no more a possibility than forward. I had only onward.

Would I miss Baby? No. Baby was a disappointment, shriveled and prosaic. She had passed through my body like any other indigestible calcium. Would I miss Charlie Chaplin? No. He was only ever a substitute. When you go running from your sex fiend father, where else do you run but into the arms of a pedophile movie star? I should have shot my father when I had the chance and gone to jail and sold cigarettes to real killers and written books about it and been canonized for my troubles. I could have been a prisoner of war. I could have been a petty thief and a homosexual. Only I was forever in the wrong place at the wrong time, so all I got to be was a mother. Yeah, right.

Part Two:
Gone Too Far

Cemetery Gates

The ghost of Sisterhood haunted me. She chased bones through my dreams as far as Italy, and she dug up my father's corpse and humped it. She brought me bits of his decomposing body and offered me a trial subscription to *Horny Pregnant Babes*, allowing me to read for free for six months, which was really an offer too good to be missed. Sisterhood would look at me mournfully in my dreams and recite Byron, Shelley, and Keats from memory, which was ironic, because when she was alive, I had trouble persuading her to put down her doggy chews and even pick up a book!

Then Sisterhood started appearing to me in my waking life, dressed in a different Halloween costume each time. She had a strange sense of humor. For the first visitation she wore a pumpkin suit that was quite adorable and told me to always remember that two wrongs don't make a right. The next time she was dressed as Dorothy from *The Wizard of Oz* and insisted that I buy her cigarettes from the bodega because she didn't have her fake ID with her. She even had a miniature Toto doll in her basket, which I thought was a very authentic touch; and she wore a wig with plaited pigtails. On the third visitation she said absolutely nothing and was dressed as Scooby-Doo.

She didn't leave. She has been floating behind me ever since, levitating, undead, undog, undone. If I forget to keep track of her in this mini-series, it's not because she's unimportant; it's just that she has taken on the psychic qualities of wallpaper now, however gruesome and phantasmagoric. A lot of homosexual couples have a dog instead of children, and I was one of those couples. I attended a séance in Alabama. I approached a priest to exorcise her in Alameda. I absolved myself of guilt for her death after a visit to the Rin Tin Tin memorial bandstand in Arkansas, and thus she finally took me back into her confidences. She took off her Scooby Doo costume, too; though I really wish she hadn't, because as it came off, its absence revealed the gaping bullet wound right between the eyes, where I had shot her. My three-eyed ghost dog and I—a pleasure to meet you I'm sure—sang sea-shanties and marched together—making no reference verbal or otherwise to the occasion of her death. It was water under the bridge, and the dry blood in her fur and the scabby, pus-filled gash in her head only occasionally oozed, only very slightly spilt her brains on the ground for her very own edible delectation.

In the summer of my twenty-third birthday, in a graveyard in Turin, the Virgin appeared to me in cornflower blue, and spoke nothing. Radiant, she simply pointed toward a hulking limestone angel (in loving memory of Man Queen, born 1882, died 1982) and nodded, "Yes," before she vaporized like the azure smoke from a joint. After falling to my knees in disbelief (I could not believe I had met our Holy Mother without my Garfield autograph book!) and cycling through all seven stages of grief in under six minutes, I crawled through the grass on my stomach. Sisterhood was circling the appointed grave, eyeballing the corroded angel, pumping it for information. Like the serpent winding toward the Fall of Man, I approached, heard a soft sob, and withdrew in waiting.

Behind the statue sat a little pink drag queen, doing bumps of coke off a fresh headstone; smoother you see, easier to snort from. She looked at me unalarmed, friendly, beckoned me over and asked if I'd like to try. *Well*, I thought, *I've given birth, been ditched by my lover, seen the Virgin Mary, patched up relations with my dead dog, and abandoned my baby daughter today. I think I could use a bit of blow. I deserve it!*

I snorted heavily with a fifty-euro bill up my right nostril. Blood trickled out of my left nostril, and the drag queen said, "I'm a lesbian, and my name's Candy Bar. What's yours?"

"Diana," I replied.

"Yeah, you look like you could be a Diana. More?" she said, gesturing to the white pile.

"Sure."

We hoovered mounds of cocaine off gravestones all afternoon, and we told each other all our favorite secrets. It happened on the spot, born not in a manger but in a graveyard. We had been hammered out as a pair by a sweet-natured blacksmith, who slipped diamonds of altruism into his mundane workload of bloody shackles and murderous pokers. Why did I love her? Because she was unspoiled and she cherished me. She saw me as fully formed, not as a manuscript full of incomplete sentences. She believed that I existed and was unafraid to put her fingers into my weeping gashes, to acknowledge that pain. I was high when I told her every-thing—like, really high—and I told her *everything*. Maybe it was uncalled for, but I threw before her the story of that night, when I was thirteen and unprotected. The coke made me more arch than usual. I had no remorse for my former self, for the brutalized me; and I spoke of her with contempt, as if I must abuse her more, keep her at arms length to prevent the shame that oozed from her from infecting me.

"I woke up in the middle of a dream about Saint Fran-cesca, a secretary I canonized on behalf of the Church, who were busy at the time casting for the lead role in their new movie musical. The dream was really enjoyable, but waking up wasn't because my father was trying to stick his limp dick in me. I had this stuffed elephant called Myra on the bed, and I asked, 'Doesn't this motherfucker know how to please a lady?'

And Myra says, "Bitch, please." She'd seen it all before, said she'd never found a man who could even approximate her desires. 'I'd rather jerk off alone than waste my time un-der a sack of shit like him.'"

I wanted to point out that I didn't exactly have a choice in the matter, but my father had a very tight hold on my skull and it was all starting to get painful. He didn't exactly pen-etrate me but rather lay his full weight on me, and I felt that my hips would break for sure. I could hear them creaking like an old steamship and I imagined, envisioned, was washed up in, a sensation of feeling them splinter. I started to squirm, I couldn't catch my breath, I wanted to cry out, "Daddy!" but I knew that was bound to make the old bastard hard as a rock. I tried to kick him in the balls, I tried to gouge tear tracks into his cheeks with my press-on nails, but they snapped off with the pressure.

"Shitty dollar-store cosmetics!" I coughed, and a little bit of blood came up from somewhere with my words.

"Tell me about it," says Myra.

I tried to twist, I tried to turn, I tried to beg, I tried to loosen his grip, I tried to scream and prayed to Saint Francesca that her severed hand might reanimate and rip my father's dick from his torso. No such luck.

My father kept on creating friction between our bodies, dragging himself over me like cheese on a grater; and I, the duplicitous traitor, stretched out beneath him on the rack with my bones in agony. I started to get wild. I started to think the vilest thoughts I could in the hope that I would spontaneously combust, go up in a huge fireball and take this bony bastard with me. But nothing I could conjure matched the horror of my current actuality. I started chanting to myself:

My father is raping me, my father is raping me, my father is raping me. I am thirteen and my father is raping me, I am thirteen and my father is raping me, I am thirteen and my father is raping me, I am thirteen and my father is raping me.

It became like a prayer, or rather, a spell, or rather, what's the difference? I heard that people become possessed during moments of great trauma, that they lose their minds and their strength doubles, and that they go on violent rampages. But nothing happened.

I remember asking my bedroom, "If this is not a moment of great trauma, what the fuck is?"

"Honeydarlingangelsweetiebabychild," said Myra, "don't sweat it. You can always repress this later on, and it'll hardly never bother you again every day."

"I'm too old for a teddy bear," I said and knocked her from the bed.

As she fell from the top bunk, past the middle bunk (where my brother slept before he killed himself), past the bottom bunk (where my father slept when he wasn't raping me), and onto the cheaply carpeted floor, Father shot his hot load all over the entrance to my vagina. There was a lot of cum, and I almost felt proud, you know? But I refrained from cheering, "Go, Dad!" He massaged my labia, smearing his sperm all over them, until they glistened like honey buns. Then, deliberately, skillfully, mercilessly, he picked up a whole handful of sperm , which he thrust violently into my cunt. I screamed. I screamed loudly and with such intensity that I almost passed out. I had never felt such an almighty pain in my life, my father's brilliant, hot semen was three fingers deep into my body. He had given those tadpoles a helping hand, and that's where Baby came from, though she's more than just wet sperm now—she's a thing. And when he finished, he rolled off and went to buy himself a bottle of ginger ale."

Candy Bar would have wept if she could have, but that wasn't her style. In silence, she took the candyfloss wig from her head and held it in front of her face, regarding it regally; then crowned me with it. She took my hand and kissed it tenderly. "La Diana," she said, "daughter of the moon. You shall *totally* ascend."

It was always like that with Candy Bar. She was a quiet, affirmative soothsayer. When I saw her I heard the Shire-lles sing. She had lived and wasn't rotten; she had plumbed depths and had not lost her soul. She was a child in chains, always on the brink of transcendence, with that Benzedrine daze on her face, her wig perpetually sliding backward, and a fluttering of her eyelids that threatened to sever the lovely little gossamers that tethered her to this life. Sometimes when I think of her now, I weep tears of lip-gloss.

We read comic books as the clouds flirted overhead. It was a lot of fun. When the sun got too hot and the coke high too intense, Candy Bar unfurled a parasol and gave me an ice cube to suck on. Inside it was a tiny, orange crystallized scorpion, and as the ice melted it began to reanimate. Tiptoe-ing down my tongue with a tiny torchlight, the scorpion sent a shaft of light down my throat and hollered, "All clear!" (in a voice many times bigger than its minute body), then disap-peared down my esophagus. I felt the ticklish little footsteps descend deep into my body, and the scorpion splashing about in the juices of my stomach, reminding me of Baby's impa-tient moods. The sensation grew until I was hiccupping wild-ly, feeling a rush of pins and needles all over my body, climax-ing in a gargantuan sneeze that propelled the scorpion out of my nose and into the air, trailing a sparkling banner of white crystals behind it and yelling, "Yippee ki-yay motherfucker!"

Candy Bar was well stocked for an afternoon in the graveyard; amongst her picnic baskets and home hair-dye kits, she had a braided garlic necklace and an Easy-Bake oven. She yanked off a bulb of garlic and popped it into the oven to roast. Out of the plastic pink mouth of the tacky little stove came a seductive, only slightly threatening voice. "*Good morning, Vietnam!*" came the familiar intonation of the murder bush...

> *You are listening to Tropicalia FM! It's another bright and breezy day here in the sunny Federal Republic! Despite last night's incredible mudslides, which unfortunately demolished one hundred thousand homes, the sun has come out to shine down on Diana and her all-important mission. Surely she's the luckiest girl alive! After getting sidetracked at an all-you-can-eat pizza buffet just outside Florence, our heroine finds herself behind schedule, having forgotten to replace the batteries in her radio alarm clock. Doesn't she know she's on a mission? Why, just last week, having overslept again, she found herself fleeing a necrophiliac tax advisor and leaped out a fourth-floor window, fortunately landing on a giant inflatable hamburger, which had been installed earlier that day to promote the opening of a new diner. Such serendipity can't always be relied upon, however, and when the clock is ticking...*

I slammed the Easy-Bake oven closed. I was feeling anxious. The murder bush was harshing my mellow. I wasn't finding her overbearing omnipotence such a great comfort any longer.

"Wow," said Candy Bar, "you're like a movie star or

something."

"Uh-uh," I said, "I'm the daughter of the Apocalypse."

"Cool!" she replied.

"I don't know. I'm not sure I'm up to the job."

"You can to-tally do that, Diana, I can to-tally help you do that, Diana, we can *totally* do that!" said Candy Bar, high as a kite.

And right there we made a pact to kick the world full in the skull and ram its head into the toaster, to make breakfast from its face, and Candy Bar promised to help me end the world. In the protracted sunlight, we admired the dancing tombstones rehearsing for the new Busby Berkeley picture, *Grave Diggers of 1933*. It was cute, and we yawned together. When we started to shake and come down, we held each other tightly in the long grasses of the churchyard, staring at the sky, eyes burning with the desperate hope that the Virgin Mary might appear to us again. She did not (but she's a working mother and we understood the many demands on her time).

If You Lay the Number Eight on Her back You Have Infinity.

Candy Bar and I were magic. She was all press-on nails and polyester pleats and synthetic beehive wigs, and she found the real her at a Madonna concert, quite by chance. With Candy Bar it was always sunshine, it was always brunch, it was always sherbet. We sat around the graveyard for a long time, practically the whole day, with the spirit of Sisterhood swooping above our heads, shooting up and hiccupping. The graveyard was gold leaf and gilt, every little corner was rococo splendor, and the grass was beveled. The tombstones carried turquoise portraits of the Bourbon dynasty, the Ming dynasty, the Tudors, the Barrymores, and the Kennedys. Mausoleums poured out sunshine thick as honey; the dead can dance and they do. They came out of their hiding holes and grooved around a campfire with their love beads clattering against their thoracic cages. They wore bandanas and clapped their hands, and shook their tambourines. They dragged deep on fat spliffs, and got real close to each other, sometimes laughing uncontrollably, sometimes running their bony fingers over each other's clavicles, along the sternum, down the spine, over the pelvis, skull on skull, tongueless mouths kissing, ribs interlocking in a skeletal love orgy.

Candy Bar said, "Hey! Let's go on a treasure hunt."

We ran around the streets of Los Angeles, from thrift store to bathhouse, looking for clues. We had our names tattooed on the inside of our wrists so that when we held hands our names made out. Candy Bar and I thought things over: what would two single girls do, alone in the world without any savings? Candy Bar suggested we go into policing or politics, but I have always been averse to concealed cash transactions. I have always wanted to live exposed, with the wind blowing right through me and the sun bleaching my bones. Living in spite of myself, and spitting in anyone's face if they even dare to doubt my absolute right to brilliance, sparkling and reflecting and dazzling and keeping myself clean of all the scum that coats everybody else in this bog of a world. Candy Bar understood, and her eyes misted somewhat, but she was butch enough to hold it together and said that she would go out into the world and make money for us. Candy Bar used to work in a department store, before the effects of the late nuclear fallout forced everyone out of the cities and all the merchandise there became totally worthless.

At her counter, Candy Bar would select colors and crèmes for her extravagant clientele and slap their faces with them. She'd take the lonely spinsters, and the doddering mothers of preeminent Nazis and the mousy secretaries and make whores of them all, with just a few flicks of her palate. She painted on grotesque, cavernous, carnivorous mouths that dripped hot, wet blood like a cunt shedding itself, or like an abortion or a botched hysterectomy. Mouths that no man would ever approach with an erection, mouths that would devour. Candy Bar painted on eyes, huge, omnipotent eyes in green, the eyes of a monster that lurked in dungeons, waiting. Candy Bar gave them cheeks like welts from chemical burns, so that their jawbones had the appearance of breaking the skin, and so that these women's skulls would appear to tear through their own flesh and eat their own faces.

With a final flourish, Candy Bar would spritz her client in a mist of some mysterious, potent pheromone that only attracted cobras and hyenas, and sigh with joy. Stunned (as a person on the receiving end of a sharp blow to the front of the skull often is), these women would inevitably shriek in utter, utter horror and then buy everything. And Candy Bar would wrap it all meticulously and tot up her commission as she did, and as an extra something, would sprinkle crushed glass into each vial of cosmetics.

Often, as her clients left the department store, Candy Bar would hear cars brake and passersby scream, and the occasional gunshot; and she would feel proud and daydream of those bloody faces, those disengaged eyeballs, those lacerated cheeks oozing before mirrored dressing tables all over Chicago, and all thanks to her.

Of course, all of the department stores were abandoned now. Only the lowest of the low, nuns, priests, and apostles lived in them now. Taking shelter from the hollow sky and the relentless assaults on streetwalkers from long-range homemade missiles launched from sentry towers and designed to keep spirituality where it belongs, in the supermarket. Department stores were now ghettoes for the holy. Inside them stood great big gleaming altars made from endless shirt boxes stood end-on-end and decorated with an eternity of cut-crystal perfume bottles. Crying out to a god who had forgotten them, or who never knew them, His servants called for deliverance or acceptance into the next life, the afterlife, life after death, instead of this death in life and abandonment.

The Church had officially denounced all practitioners of the faith as heretics, after undoing the existence of every saint whoever preached peace, justice, or consideration to man or beast. They excommunicated Christ for being a faggot, Mary for being a hooker, and Joseph for being a pedophile and a rapist, then systematically euthanized every Bishop who voted against the proposal to reduce overheads by merging with Hinduism. (As it turned out, the rights to Lord Shiva were already owned by Disney, the Church's rival theme park, so the deal went to shit.) The Church now existed solely to promote its line of watches produced under license wherever they could be manufactured cheapest. They all bore the face of Pope Alexander VI, who was commonly regarded as the only person fit for the position of head of the Church, being that he was undoubtedly one of the most debased killers of all time.

Attempts to bring His Holiness back from the dead at first looked good. It was thought he could at least be revived as part cyborg, if nothing more suitable could be arranged. However, those of us who remembered the Pope's first rampage in the fourteenth century were quite adamant that this not happen, and we plotted against him. For the second time, Alexander was sent back into the ground after somebody switched his carburetor for the cooling element from a fridge freezer and he blew up at his coronation.

The Pope's face on a sports watch was a fitting tribute, thought the Camerlengo as he signed over the Church to the exclusive control of IBM, shortly before being knifed to death. The college of Cardinals sold off the Vatican for enormous personal profits. They sobbed amongst each other about the situation coming to this—shortly before they were castrated and garroted. Had they retained the support of the magical beasts and beings on whom the power of the Church had always rested, they wept, things might have been different. The Cardinal from Antigua cried, "If only we still had the transsexuals on our side." Then somebody from Microsoft ripped his guts out with the claw of a hammer.

After the economy ate itself, everybody else in need of funding simply took to highway robbery, holding people up at knifepoint on street corners. Sadly, there was little money to be extracted from anyone, and since everyone was armed and a mugger the stolen money went around and around, an endless refrain, between thief and victim, victim and thief.

I suggested we turn tricks, but Candy Bar pointed out we'd fucked everyone for free already, that we were in fact saturated with sex in a market saturated with sex. So we lay down again on our mattress, which was soaked thick with cum, and we thought. Or rather, thoughts spilt out our ears, we let our minds become soft, aching blanks in the hope that ideas and inspirations would run right through them like the Midnight Express. July's heavy, volcanic sunbeams scorched our bodies in their denim cut-offs and their bikini tops, their sundresses and tennis shoes. Popsicles melted in our sticky hands as we emptied our brains onto the sidewalk of L.A.

What did we even need money for? We hardly ever ate anything at all, and all our drugs were free; and since we (being women) were ineligible to vote, we weren't obliged to pay taxes. Being dead, Sisterhood didn't need to be fed, and Baby had not caught up with me to push for paternity payouts, so our only real overheads were the insect repellent and the razor blades we bought from the last pharmacy on the corner that hadn't fallen into rebel hands—yet. But it was more than that; our desire for money was a primordial instinct, a desperation, a want that could only be settled the hard way. No amount of fucking and no amount of freedom and no amount of coke up the cunt could quench it. We needed fur coats in the midday sun, enormous sleek cars for which all fuel had long since seeped away, diamonds besmirched with bloody little fingerprints to fill the gaps where our teeth had fallen out from eating too many donuts.

A long funeral procession came past us, banging drums as loud as all hell, mourners crying by the hour, and everyone dressed in purple, the color of sexual frustration (well, would you fuck a corpse?).

"Would you fuck a corpse?" I asked Candy Bar.

"Probably, if she was cute."

"Could I watch?" I asked.

She licked the coke residue from my armpits and said, "Don't be dirty."

I watched the funeral procession disappear slowly and noisily toward the haunted house on the hill as Sisterhood howled along off-key (the poor bitch is tone deaf, to add to her troubles). There were rumors that the mad scientist who worked up there with the vampiric landlord took in fresh corpses and made them into macaroni for disadvantaged school children in inner cities, but I didn't believe it. No one was that charitable. They said that the vampire in question was Dracula himself, my all-time favorite movie star (well, at least since I broke up with Charlie Chaplin). I longed to go to the castle, stroke the pet tarantulas, walk through the cemetery, slide along the secret passages, and throw myself about on Dracula's big, crushed velvet bed. I imagined Dracula approaching me in an unquenchable fit of lust and how I'd make Dracula beg for it.

The presence of the mad scientist puzzled me a little, though. (Dracula is eternally chic, but his pal's archetype surely went out of fashion with Frank Sinatra; then again, what do I know? I'm just a girl from the sticks.) Maybe they came together in a gift set. Perhaps they were picked up in a buy-one-get-one-free special offer, or they were lovers. I couldn't say; economics never was my thing. L.A. always begged to make sense, and I missed Berlin.

I thought for a while about a vampire I had known when I was growing up on the farm. He hummed opera when he gave me head, before my father had ever raped me. I thought that was what sex was, a boy putting his head between your legs and making you squirm and telling you that you were pretty. When my father told me he wanted to fuck me, I said, "Okay," so maybe it wasn't technically rape, although I did scream, "No! No! No!" when I realized what he really meant, and I did kick and did try to fight him off, and I did lose that round. I wondered if my tween vampire lover had ever swallowed any of my blood, and I wondered if that counted, whether I was now immortal, whether I could go run in front of a truck just for kicks and bounce off the windscreen.

I could start a lucrative insurance scam in which I constantly faked my own death. Candy Bar and I could get very rich very easily. Seeing as how less than a third of the world's population had survived, insurance companies were practically flooded with unclaimed dividends from whole extended families who'd been well covered but were wiped out. I could take out seventy-seven policies and fake my own death several times over and spend all the money on laxatives, so I could gorge myself on fine French cheeses and never have to worry about slowing down. With that much money, I could make it an art project, I could make it a gallery piece, a cult classic, a ready-to-wear installation. I could insist people only talk to me in capital letters. I could buy up old titles from long-since-murdered noble families and string all my names together until they filled three notepads full of loose-leaf paper and everyone had to wait at the door for two days for me to be fully announced. I'd buy every book in the world and cut out every reference to the protagonist and replace that name with mine: Diana. And Diana would pull the sword from the stone, and Diana would wrack herself with guilt over King Duncan and ache for Genji and Heathcliff, and Diana would journey to the ends of the Earth, and Diana would wear the scarlet letter *A*, and Diana would kill an old pawnbroker and hack up her hookers.

But before I even signed my name on the dot-dot-dotted

line of the first insurance policy, Candy Bar grabbed me by the arm and insisted we run downtown. She said she'd gotten me a much better job. I wasn't going to be a prostitute or a policeman or the girl behind the make-up counter or a conman or a priest or immortal or a vampire slayer or a TV host or a terrorist or a mannequin or a fire fighter or a freedom fighter, not Angela Davies, not Joan of Arc, not PJ Harvey, and not Charlemagne, but some mixture of the lot.

After hearing me sing in the bathtub, Candy Bar had taken it upon herself to find me a job as a nightclub singer, somewhere very smoky where everybody was bisexual and drank too much. Diazepam Nite Spot was the only place the demimonde was ever to be seen. It's where heiresses to nothing and playboys with erectile dysfunctions went to be louche in their threadbare suits and drink watered-down martinis, and now I was to be their new star. I wondered if I would see Thackeray there, but I never did. The previous singer had taken a wrong turn off the end of the pier after an argument with the bar's owner, The Tsar—too bad. People said that she was really Billie Holiday, trying one last time to go clean; people said I had big shoes to fill. (I always hated that expression, and anyway, I wear a size 44.)

Optimism

As we ran downtown toward Diazepam Nite Spot, all the way through Manhattan, over the debris of billboards, condominiums, meteorites, Church bells, and burnt out delicatessens, with Sisterhood yelping at our heels, I asked Candy Bar a question. She knew the answer.

"Have you noticed anything different about me lately?"

"You mean your balls? That's life Diana, the body changes, you know?"

A transsexual adolescent reveals herself where and when she will. I was in my mid-twenties now. I was a boy now. My hair had grown short now. I had masculine musculature now. My cock was visible now, pressed against the silk of my kimono dress (Candy Bar and I never wore underwear).

"I literally do not care what's in your trousers," Candy Bar continued, slightly out of breath. "You're the air, I'm the air, that old lady is the air, and half a dozen oysters down in Acapulco are the air."

I felt comforted. Candy Bar was so wise.

We stopped at the base of some famous monument, some rock star's mansion, some historical garden, some something. We ordered two cherry brandies with lemonade from the ice cream parlor, from the man with the terrible affected British accent and the big, bright, white, gleaming teeth like piano keys. I wanted to play his mouth. I wanted to bash out my feelings (as they used to be called in the soap operas before the revolution) on the keys, roll up my shirt sleeves, push the hair out of my eyes in frustration, chain-smoke, knock back whiskies, and just hammer out that melody all night long until it was ready to be recorded. Recorded by The Shirelles, maybe, oh, imagine! Writing for The Shirelles! Sweating, nervously dabbing at my brow at an award show, awaiting the opening of that envelope and the announcement of who had won Best Vocal Recording by a Female or Other *Untermensch*. Touring Cuba. Accused of being a Red. Blacklisted. White out.

Candy Bar rolled my glass down the bar to me and smiled her wondrous smile that told of the edge coming off an anxiety attack, a hard day at the office overcome by just one little blue pill that gave her a hard-on in her will to live.

"Cheers!"

We necked our cherry brandy and lemonades, and then we necked with each other. I felt a little like I imagined Shirley Temple felt when she gave her name to that silly dry-state cocktail. Then I thought of Mrs. Molotov and how much prouder she must have felt upon the christening of her cocktail, over the head of the White army, over the head of the Nazi army, over the head of the Cheka, over the head of a statue of Stalin that stood in the village square. The genius of fire made portable, bettered only by napalm, that divine body lotion capable of wiping away all your tears by burning away all your flesh.

I was a little drunk, but Candy Bar said I'd need some

fortifications to deal with The Tsar, if I weren't to crumble under the touch of the lecherous old devil. And he was a devil. Not *the* devil, but *a* devil, one of Satan's angels recommended for high rank in the military or the government, who had ignored the callings of high office in favor of the attractions of running a dirty little nightclub, where he could preside like Lucifer himself (of whom he'd always been so terribly jealous, and on whom he'd always had an enormous crush, obviously). I opened the door.

Diazepam Nite Spot was exactly what it should have been, or else why would I have been there? The same people sat there all night and all day, dolled up like interwar movie stars, surrounded by coils of sculptural cigarette smoke unfurling like ivory calligraphy. The bar was well stocked and dimly lit, a mustached bartender polished glasses, cigarette girls sold smokes and handjobs, every face was painted white and rouged at the cheeks, and the place smelt like decadence gone sour. Everyone was shown in silhouette, angular, expensive, feathered, bejeweled like the court of Elizabeth I, and I wanted to cry out in joy and disgust, having found what I was looking for and been horrified by it.

Funny then, how previously the corpses, the gunfights, the zombies, the rapes, the dead dogs, the grandmothers bleeding to death in the street, the decapitations of priests, the buildings collapsing on accordion players, the crucifixions, and the suicide bombings in the name of the Father, the Son, and the Holy Ghost had all failed to provoke anything in me but a mild dislike. I was prepared for my dealings with the devil; in truth I hoped that this wicked man might bring me closer to the knowledge of how I was meant to euthanize the planet.

The Tsar was a corpulent fellow who collected Disney figurines, half James Bond villain, half Mother Goose. He was not unlikeable, but I did dislike him deeply. He hired me as a nightclub singer on the spot, and I was born onto the stage as a dubious starlet.

As a child I would sit in front of the phonograph and listen over and over and over to the lacerating, snarling, and indefinable voice of my favorite singer, Justine Bondage. At age five I would dress up like her (my father called me a lesbian), sit up all night listening to her old recordings from the Royal Variety Command Performance in 1947, trying to get my hair to rise like hers. Whenever she was on the black-and-white television set, I was immovable. I could quote her, and I would dress up Sisterhood like her, too. I watched Justine sing in French and make up the words as the department of subtitles scrambled to translate her message, which was impossible because she was beyond words, even if you did speak that nonexistent language, which nobody did (though Baby had always claimed she was "proficiently conversational" in it).

When she took the stage, Justine strode, her blond bangs held in place by a crown of stars, her eyes flashing green glitter on green, green irises, and she sucked in all the air in the room. Her audience suffocated with desire, mesmerized, or at least that's how I explained their crawling, their scrambling across the floor and down the aisles toward her with bouquets and proposals and white wedding hats. Sometimes she cried on stage; maybe her own magnificence was too much. I knew that she was haunted. She was visited by ghosts on her stage, old friends, old rivals, and later by the undead of AIDS, and those she had killed with her own hands in barroom brawls. Justine liked to drink, and her kisses were always tinted so softly with gin, the drink of abortionists and miscalculations and abandoned dreams and lost opportunities and the determination to get it right this time.

As a child there was only one Justine Bondage; in my adolescence she had remained. Someone told me she had once been a resistance fighter, and not just a foot soldier, but the commander of a battalion in Belgium; and I didn't doubt it. I would leave messages for her on every bathroom wall I visited. I would scrawl questions in magic marker. I would ask her for advice, or I would try to express my confusion, and she would sometimes respond. Once she wrote me one single glistening word on the white tiles of an ultra, ultra, uber, uber, fancy, fancy hotel: "Optimism." I crossed myself and ran my hand across that still wet ink, but it didn't smudge. It merely transferred itself onto my torso, and I wear it now as a tattoo over my heart without a dagger running through it. I did up my zipper and stepped away from the urinal, as always feeling the slightest wetness roll down my urethra and into my trousers.

Thus Candy Bar dressed me for my debut, my gala premiere, in a black cocktail dress with armored puffs at the shoulders, a gown pulled all tight over my body. It was Lycra, opaque cellophane, a snake's skin, and it was deathly chic and deathly perfect for the audience of rich corpses who sat through the dinner theater at Diazepam Nite Spot every evening. I looked into the mirror, and I was a boy in a dress, as I had been a boy in a girl the day before; and the day after I would be Katharine Hepburn again, a girl in slacks. Candy Bar massaged my shoulders, stoned. Her eyes were rolling in her head. The stage manager had smoked her out, she powdered my face to clean off the shine. I shouldn't look shiny, I shouldn't look as though my body functioned, I shouldn't shit onstage.

I laughed. When Candy Bar was stoned she was always so wildly happy, maniacally so. She was no paranoid stoner, no therapy drunk, no speed victim, though coke did make her edgy, and many times before now I had had to play her *The Sound of Music* to calm her down. I hate Julie Andrews. The nuns and the Nazis are the same, as Holly Hughes told me once at a rave. Mary Jane made Candy Bar joyous, and that made me joyous; but I went onstage to spit at my audience out of fear, out of desire, out of frustration and anxiety and longing.

Every night before I went on, the emcee would tell the same seven jokes, each one bawdier, each one less funny, each one step closer to the Apocalypse, and with each one I exhaled the wish that this would be the night we saw the end of the world. All the world is a stage, and this stage was a battleship with a skeleton crew, adrift in the freezing Atlantic; for the Bermuda Triangle would have been too sunny of a mercy. Diazepam Nite Spot was a floating pleasure palace and always full of seamen, at the back, in standing room only, behind our monocled and pearled clientele, many of whom

Candy Bar recognized from the department store. She'd wave to them and ask how they'd liked the eye shadows and face creams she had prescribed, and invariably they'd rave about the virtues of the products (with the scars and wounds still visible on their faces) and offer Candy Bar a drink. Invariably, she'd come backstage rolling drunk and smirk, "La Diana, I love you."

"Well I love you, too, Princess," I'd say and mean it, and I'd hold her hand like she was my sister and I was walking her to school.

The sailors wore white high-waisted bellbottoms and white muscle vests and little white caps, tilted like yachts themselves. They were uproarious, animalistic, visceral, charming, and alive; and the pianist had a hard-on for them. They came into the club in packs, on leave from the hulking destroyers that were moored outside in the saturated-pink sunlight. They ordered by the bottle, which thrilled The Tsar, and they were always drunk and always wanting to fuck, and Candy Bar thought that she could pimp me out to them for a good price. I wasn't interested.

The sailors were loyal. They had nowhere else to go, and their leave had been extended from days to weeks to months to years to decades; and they lived on in a permanent, horny, boring reverie, growing no older, just more tan, forever nineteen, which made me the older woman. The sailors roared through my set every night. Some timidly gave me chocolates in heart-shaped boxes. If ever a member of the audience, in black and seated, dared to express disinterest with so much as a yawn during my performance, then there was trouble. I repaid the sailors by taking the time to walk amongst them, with the spotlight following me around the club. I would take a flower out of my hair, smell it, and then hand it over to one of the boys, who roared all the more. Roared like cannon fire or dogfights over England deciding empires in decline.

Querelle stood head and shoulders above the rest because he was a thief and a poet, and a distraction from my more real feelings, those that I carried around in my jewelry box, as precious as diamonds and more torturously extracted. Those feelings for the pianist. The pianist liked me, had very broad shoulders and was very decent, almost loving; but to him I was not a strapping sailor. I was just a girl—or a boy in a dress. Who knows? He would greet me warmly and hold me with a tenderness and affection that I occasionally mistook for longing; and then I would go back to my room and smash everything to infinitesimal pieces and scream, and curse my old French maid, and lunge with intent at Sisterhood, who vaporized in fear. Then I sobbed with my face pressed against a mirror so I could see exactly how pathetic I was. I think it was in just such a situation that Querelle found me, and so I toyed with him for a while, which was cruel; but I thought he was a joke at first, and I needed so badly to be amused. Fame had isolated me.

Querelle was famous for fucking everyone. His persistence was incredible, and so he fucked me, or rather, I fucked him, repeatedly, or rather, someone's dick was in someone's asshole and the specifics are irrelevant and annoying. All there is to say is that I didn't fall in love with Querelle, and he didn't fall in love with the pianist, but the pianist did fall in love with him, and it all ended very badly, because I loved the pianist and the pianist loved Querelle, who I think maybe had been in love with me, and oh what the fuck did it matter? I smashed more bottles.

I screamed at the maid some more, and Candy Bar tried to understand, she honestly did; but I was under contract and alone and went back onstage in a loveless marriage with the pianist, the two of us tied back-to-back to a rock with the tide coming in around us. Drowning is not a peaceful death. It's slow and painful, not poetic, not dreamlike. It feels like suffocation and panic, terror, terror, terror, the kind you can only ever experience once in your life, after which you're broken. Dying is easy. It's living that scares me to death. Drowning is not a peaceful death. Ask the sailors, they know.

On my days off from singing cabaret to the undead elites of uptown I spent my time ashore in the tearooms of Great Britain. Sometimes Candy Bar came with me, but usually she spent her time dressed as a secretary and rented out her photocopier on the street corner. She was of an independent mind, always enterprising; and besides, she had acquired a taste for the kind of ketamine you had to pay for. Amongst the dowagers and the unemployed, I sat days on end, barely conscious and stirring sugar into my tea, dropping broken pieces of stale cookies on the floor for Sisterhood to gobble, endlessly dreaming of snow. It never snows in New York anymore. It's always too cold, so we all have to pretend and make do with polystyrene ice shelves and their shavings and Styrofoam peanuts. If it did snow, I'd know Baby was coming back home. She wouldn't dare arrive with an entrance less dramatic than a blizzard, now that her mother was a bonafide star below 14th street. I wondered if I missed her, wondered who changed her diapers. I wondered, *Is she being brought up in the Catholic faith, or had Thackeray just thrown her out of the car at high speed as they rounded a bend in Malibu?* It never snows in Malibu, either.

A waitress bent double, like the number seven, cleared and then filled my table, unable to exhaust herself or my own patience quickly enough. I wore very tight trousers and a fur stole; the old ladies told me that I reminded them of the punk rock stars who led the Conservative government at the turn of the century. I imagined that to be a compliment because the dowagers were smiling, at least, so I thanked them with an autograph and made a note on my napkin to research this topic more completely. Research was hard. The Internet had been uninvented shortly before the revolution, since its existence had so stupefied people as to make all political action impossible.

Ironically, deprived of social networking sites and volumes of free pornography, the people finally did revolt and began throwing up decades worth of resentment, emotional repression and class oppression all over the kitchen floor. Soon there was so much puke clogging the drainpipes of England that even the country's notoriously slow and clumsy plumbers could do nothing about it, so the puppet government (which was actually comprised of a handful of sock puppets and a few moth-eaten Punch-and-Judy dolls) declared marshal law, fled to Australia (where at least it was warm) and left the country in the hands of Admiral Duncan.

Books had also been banned, or rather, had banned themselves, since publishers refused to print anything other than the classics they already owned the rights to, or guides to interior design that the advertising sales team mocked up during their lunch breaks, whilst fingering each other. Information had to a great degree stopped flowing. It's true that text messages were still popular even after the revolution; but since there was no electricity anymore, there were soon no working cellphones either.

If a person wanted to find anything out these days, she had to go to Blackpool and walk to the end of the pier where she would find the Oracle, rolling on acid and predicting the future. The Oracle was dedicated to and in the service of Apollo, the God of tragic space launches, and you could ask the Oracle any question you wanted to. Except one. You could not ask the Oracle:

"Oracle, when will the world end?"

Because the Oracle would not tell you, would ignore your question; and since the Oracle answered all questions, your question did not exist. I drew all over the tearoom table-cloth. I drew the Oracle and the Oracle's visions; the sketches became one enormous line drawing, a family tree. I had visited the Oracle and had asked a question. What it was escapes me now, but that is not the interesting part of the recollection anyhow.

I took the bus to Blackpool one gray Tuesday, and I hung around the stage door at the end of the pier, hoping to get Justine Bondage's autograph when she came out after her famed weekly consultation. Everybody knew she always saw the Oracle on a Tuesday, right after she had her hair done, so I waited, but she did not materialize. Instead, when the door finally swung open, I was face to face with the Oracle.

The Oracle, dressed in silver spandex like an ice skater, a movie musical or the future of the 1970s, stepped outside to have a fag. The Oracle exhaled. "Showbiz, eh?" The Oracle said that the Oracle could tell I was in the business too, so didn't mind sharing a few family secrets, offered me a drag on the oracular cigarette. The Oracle was flirting with me, and I played it cool. The Oracle was undoubtedly attractive and I asked:

"When will the world end?"

"Oh gee," said the Oracle, "you know, everyone wants to know that. But I just don't know, I'm not privy to that information yet, it's still classified."

Here the Oracle gestured to the sky, by which I inferred God, by which I inferred Apollo.

"All I can say is soon, God, I hope it's soon. We're all just sitting around here, aren't we? Waiting. Sandwiched between the revolution and the Apocalypse. It's too, too tragic. Say, er, kid, do you wanna fuck?"

I nodded yes, and the Oracle led me to an end-of-the-pier clam shack. In the drizzle I put my hands into my pants and rolled back my foreskin, ran my finger over the head of my dick to check that it didn't stink, and followed the Oracle inside. Surrounded by seashells and mollusks, we did it, and it felt like I was loosing my virginity, or that I was taking the Oracle's. Dude, seriously, I fucked the future.

Bringing the House Down

Of course I had to go back to the club sooner or later. I couldn't spend my whole life in love with the Oracle, though it was tempting. We spent long, languorous afternoons laid out full length together in pleasure. Knowing the future, the Oracle knew what I wanted and gave it to me, and I in turn had to race against time to keep up with that precognitive oracular desire. One twilight, amongst coils of post-coital cigarette smoke, sitting as we were in a pool of gelatinous excretions, the Oracle modestly pulled the bed sheets up over the oracular chest and very tersely said, "Well kid, lemme tell you—I don't know when the world will end, but for what it's worth, I do know that it will be *your* choice. Now I don't want to put too much stress on you, when I know you've got that competition at the Chelsea flower show coming up, but, well, dammit, kid, I'm fond of you, kid, and I wanna be straight with you."

I thanked the Oracle for being up front, though there was no further advice given. Instead the Oracle showed me how to make cotton candy and toffee apples. The Oracle said it's good to be multi-skilled; and if the Oracle ever retrained, it would be as a shopkeeper of souvenirs or a stealth bomber pilot. The Oracle told me all that really mattered was journeys, and I had a vision of the Oracle at some point in the future, flying over the bric-a-brac stall that the Oracle owned in a parallel existence, and dropping bombs like relief parcels onto it. The Oracle would foresee all of this, and would indeed blow up on the spot, in the Temple, just as the explosives dropped by the Oracle's future self detonated in the store the Oracle owned in that parallel existence. The plane (obviously now unpiloted), would dive into the sea, shrieking, a siren to the grave. Blackpool was beautiful.

The Oracle allowed me a look inside the oracular microwave oven. As a bowl of Heinz tomato soup turned round like a ballerina in a jewelry box, warming herself under the heat lamps to a piping hot temperature, I myself saw the future. I saw Baby and I playing ball on an immaculately mowed green lawn, a discarded teddy bear cast to the side and Candy Bar in the background with Charlie Chaplin grilling hamburgers. A glamorous, if undoubtedly disturbed, middle-aged woman, somewhat overdressed, stood before the proselytizing Catholic missionaries; and Thackeray had grown a moustache. The bowl ceased its rotations, the microwave let out a piercing shriek, the Oracle withdrew the oracular lunch and the vision vanished.

"The future," gestured the Oracle.

After I left, I often thought about the Oracle and wondered if the Oracle, having the power to see the future, was capable of reviewing the past in high-definition, perfect freeze frames and torturous slow motion. I wondered if the Oracle ever played back our time together, visiting particular moments in it when the Oracle was horny. Did the Oracle ever slide oracular hands into oracular underwear and jerk off the past? Had the Oracle, in fact, having the power to see the future, been jerking off over us tangled together in sweat and sea salt, before we ever even met? The ocean had come all over us, in and out all over us, high tide and low, ebbing away like our facility to stay awake any longer. I had loved the Oracle, and the Oracle had loved me; but I had a bus to catch.

I put on my cork wedges and my camel-colored overcoat and the white tennis shorts I bought from Gucci in the '70s (neither of which had been invented yet) and I headed out. The traffic was bumper to bumper, no drivers, no passengers, no engines running, just gridlocked cars lining the street as far as the eye couldn't see. I made my way between them, squeezing into the narrowest of gaps, taking the diciest of routes, in the hope I'd get pinned down amongst all that static metal. That I'd be trapped by immovable objects, and that vultures would circle overhead, swooping down once a day to give me the update on my life expectancy, with their mouths watering. I'd be good eating, I knew. I was marinated in filth, and there was no fat on me. I was prime lean, meat, and the vultures could probably sell my tennis shorts to an online sportswear enthusiast once they'd finished devouring the pearls between my legs. A skeleton sprawled pornographically on the hood of an Italian sports car was all I had ever wanted to be, and I was *this* close. Then I looked at the time, or rather, it looked at me; and, suddenly full of panic, I ran.

The streets were all uphill (something, incidentally, I also had always hated about San Francisco), and no matter how hard I tried I couldn't make any ground. The pavement, tarmac, concrete sidewalk slipped away beneath me, and I just seemed to hover in neither direction, weightless for a moment.

Later, as I approached the five-and-dime, Joan Crawford appeared in the doorway, pointed her gloved finger at me and yelled, "You! Yes, you! Has anyone ever told you that you looked like me?"

Terrified, star-struck, excited, I shook my head.

"Well, keep it that way!"

I nodded.

"Wait," she said. "Don't I know you?"

I shook my head.

"Yes I do! You're that little tramp who was fucking Charlie Chaplin, aren't you? It was all over the *Herald*! For the love of God. And you had his baby, and you ditched it with a car full of corpses somewhere in Ohio in a snowstorm, didn't you? I can't believe my eyes! Can I have your autograph?"

I nodded.

Famous people don't care about talent; that's recherché. They are much more inspired by people who became celebrities by more unconventional methods; they think it shows great initiative.

Joan Crawford had a huge autograph book bound in alligator skin, and in it were the scrawlings of so many pseudostars and upstarts—mainly serial killers (the sort who murder in terribly unusual ways), game show contestants who had won a hundred thousand dollars or so for humiliating themselves on television, the ex-lovers of folk singers who had sold their stories, and the parents of mutilated beauty queens who now advertised margarine. She was very proud of that book. I signed my name right under a former tennis pro who had hacked up his wife's lover's body with his racquet. I felt rather special. She asked me for a photograph, and I obliged; and the two of us pressed our faces together to fit into the frame of her antique cellphone camera.

"You absolutely stink of sex," said Joan Crawford. "And seafood."

I nodded my head.

She showed me the picture. We did look startlingly alike. I was thrilled.

Raindrops the size of beetles started to fall, hitting the ground with an audacious contempt. By the time I got to the club, I was soaked but clean. Sisterhood bounded over to me, jumping up excitedly to lick at my lips. Candy Bar led me by the arm to the dressing room, slapped me across the face with her open hand and started on my make-up.

"The Tsar wants you to sing *Vissi d'arte* tonight," she said as she began to backcomb my hair into a beehive like her own.

"I can't sing opera, though," I mumbled, my cheek still stinging from her welcome-home kisses.

"Well, learn! You have just under an hour; you can come up with something by then. Besides, what else have you been doing with all your time off?"

She painted my face white with a heavy grease paint. My teeth looked distinctly yellow in comparison. She whited out my eyebrows and eyelids. I became a skull with a grave for a mouth. She studded my face with pink crystals, originally intended for the decoration of office technologies, now put to better use. She stuck on false eyelashes and powdered me pink in the right places, the zinging, Technicolor pink of acid flashbacks and early Disney movies. She sprayed my hair with can after can of lacquer, smoking throughout, inches away from making a fireball of us both, a miniature Hell in the dressing room; and then she dressed me all in white. She ran twigs through my hair, bejeweled like my face. I stood up, and I was ready.

Making my way backstage toward the curtains, I could hear The Tsar himself announce me.

"This bitch has been away from our stage for three years now, and we have missed him, oh how we *have* missed her! Since she's been gone, though, rest assured, he has only become more beautiful, more talented and more charismatic—so beware. Ladies and gentlemen, good people of the underworld, the Diazepam Nite Spot is proud to present La Diana."

I went on, what else? I sang the song as requested. I knew all the words; it must have been on one of those tapes I used to play to Baby all those years ago, who knew? I sang my heart out, felt every tremor of that old melody, I *was* Maria Callas. I swallowed the microphone. It slipped down my throat and came out my ears and wrapped itself around a purely decorative pillar at the foot of the stage. Then the microphone, alive by now, or an extension of myself, began yanking harder and harder on the purely decorative pillar, until it came away from the wall and crushed a table full of patrons at their seats.

The audience roared. They stood up with tears in their eyes as the power of the aria built up, blinded by the purity of my now unamplified voice. With an almighty creak, the ceiling started to give way, as the serpentine wire, now multiplied in heads, pulled at the balustrades and the beams of the theater. My fans threw roses as the roof caved in on them. They wept and threw themselves toward the stage utterly overcome with emotion and never noticed that they were being pulverized from above by falling debris. The entire audience, the bar staff, and a few police officers were wiped out in fifteen lovely minutes.

There was soon a hole so large in the ceiling that the apartments above started sliding through like quicksand, with residents spiraling downward while still at their dinner tables, in their beds, in their bath tubs. Whole mounds of mangled bodies spread thickly across the fallen rotten wood of the former theater's former roof. The rain poured in, the water driving so hard it looked like a shipwreck (which of course it was).

Saturated, the Tsar picked through the rubble and pulled out watches, credit cards, cash and metal filings of every kind. Backstage, Candy Bar was staring in the mirror, crying.

"Diana," she sobbed when I came back, "I am *so* sorry I hit you."

All that was left was a door hanging on its hinges in what used to be its doorway.

"Goodbye, old darling," I said, stroking the poor, flimsy bit of old wood, smashed like so much flotsam.

Ten

For a while, Candy Bar and I took jobs as telephone sex operators. Apparently it is much more lucrative than actually having sex with people because johns pay by the minute, not by the cum shot, and minutes add up. They're so tiny they just slip through the fingers you wrap around your cock, and you never notice them till they're spent like your seed on the carpet.

For long days, the two of us would sit in swivel chairs, in our office overlooking the crooked city, flicking through *Women's Wear Daily*, the stylish read of choice for all whores, and moaning in a variety of manners to our customers over the phone lines. They called from all over the world, pretending it was their first time, claiming that they didn't usually do this sort of thing; or they called with bold efficiency, declaring that they knew what they wanted and how they wanted it. Occasionally, amongst the rasping, clucking, gurgling hollerings of our esteemed clientele, there would come the low, assured murmurs of the murder bush.

"Di-a-na," she said, extending the middle vowel sound of the name she had given me.

"Yes," I replied obediently.

"Just checking in…" and the receiver would clatter down

noisily, ending the call.

Pleasing men is so easy. Just pretend that you're in pain; beg them to continue, but make it sound like you want them to stop. Sometimes Candy Bar and I would switch calls mid scenario, for kicks, to see if the callers noticed the difference, and invariably they didn't.

Occasionally there would come a caller who wanted something more involved, so we would pretend we were horny pregnant babes, or schoolgirl junkies, or kinky grandmothers. Candy Bar had a real flair for it. I'd always known that shy-and-retiring bullshit was a hoax. She thought up the craziest scenarios full of horny nuns making out on riverbanks and naughty schoolboys watching from the bushes and jerking each other off! And the one about the pin-up model who takes revenge on a photographer who has humiliated her on set, and goes about victimizing him via the Royal Mail and UPS, sending him notes in newspaper collage demanding that he lick her legs like the dog he is. Or the one in which two twins separated at birth coincidentally discover their psychic capacities to sexually stimulate each other, whilst watching *Myra Breckinridge*. Now, that one was *really* great!

One afternoon, I came back from my German class and found Candy Bar in rapture, seated in her chair, rocking it wildly on its back legs, orgasming loudly with the phone to her breast. All the other girls had left for the day, it being Columbus Day and all, but Candy Bar and I were staunch anti-Imperialists so we'd stayed on. Her pink wig was slipping backward. The tiara that kept it in place had fallen to the floor, and she was spewing gold glitter and saliva from her mouth, nose and eyes, ecstatic as the Virgin Mary immaculately conceiving via phone line. She was electric and alive and fully organic, a pleasure point and the instant of her own sweet creation; and she moaned repeatedly, softly but out loud.

Acknowledging that as close as we were—sisters, lovers, mothers, brothers, users—I understood that Candy Bar deserved this moment to herself. So I chose to avert my eyes and avoid spoiling any more of this onanistic Eucharist with my gaze. On a Post-it I wrote out, *I don't fully understand this but maybe together we can work it out*. Then I stuck it on the autographed picture of the Hollywood sign that was tacked to the wall above her photocopier. Then I left the room, obviously.

I went home to the furniture salesroom where we lived, amongst the display sofas and plastic-wrapped beds some industrious billionaire had thought to turn a profit on after the projected fall of good taste, an event which sadly never came. Good taste, like cockroaches, is pervasive and indestructible. It creeps on, ever optimistic, singing *Maybe This Time*, and refusing to take a hint. Thus, after nuclear fallouts, civil wars, brilliantly executed genocides, a decade-long drought and a rampant, mutated form of semi-lethal Spanish influenza, there still remained an etiquette in interior design that posited discrete facsimiles of chintzy New England living rooms as an art form.

Amongst the hollow, unloved, washed-out fittings destined only to degrade alone in the showroom, I would wake up crying. Confused, I would reach for Baby, to protect her from the long shadow of her Grandfather, then sit up in shock and resignation, with the realization she was gone. Or rather, that I was gone. If Candy Bar was not home, Sisterhood would try to comfort me, but you just can't snuggle a phantom, and some nights I couldn't sleep at all, for fear of waking up. The threat of a new day on my shoulders was more than I could face.

When I did sleep, regaining consciousness was a grim trial. I would try to preserve the stillness and the silence as long as I could. Since I couldn't quite believe I had woken up again into this life, I wanted to maintain the illusion of the grave as long as possible. If Candy Bar were there, she would pacify me. I would cling to her humid body as if she were an island in an ocean of darkness, and I would pull myself onto her and take comfort in her smell. Often, though, she was away seducing and destroying and cataloguing life. She could not be my everything, and so I had to take heart in knowing that this loneliness would itself come to be a friend for life.

Veronica Springs Eternal

We blew town the day we heard Rudolph Valentino was dead. Candy Bar was determined to be at his funeral service. I did suggest that we ought to attend to the other mission I had been handed, but Candy Bar said it could wait.

"Besides," she reasoned, "don't you want to go to one last fabulous party before you destroy the known world? "

I had to admit that, yes, actually, I did.

"So come on then, silly, get your ass ready, we've got a train to catch!"

The body of Valentino, the world's most beautiful rapist, was being driven by steam train across the entire continent, for his endless admirers to mourn, cutting a swathe through all human life as it went. The old train moved slowly, creaking with every shunt forward; and at every stop along the way, humble people flooded the stations to pay their respects to the star, pressing themselves against his glass coffin, throwing roses, sobbing, playing violins. Such was the intensity and hysteria that greeted Valentino's train each time it pulled to a stop. The train driver (the former captain of a whaling ship) was himself utterly overcome by the outpouring of emotion and broke down at the wheel sobbing.

"Ah! It shoulda been me! He was taken from us too early,

I tell ya. Too early!"

The stewards all trembled and held back their tears with the greatest of difficulty as they walked about the train, from end to end, telling other passengers in the empty caboose that Mister Valentino was unable to lunch today. The Marie Celeste plunged through the desert, through the mountains, over great roaring rivers and barren canyons and brittle battlegrounds, and on. And all the way, the whole route, the pathway was lined with lilies that had blossomed upon hearing the saddest news, the whole curving transcontinental line written out in bloom for the blubbering train driver to follow and crush. Imagine the smell.

As the train dragged on, Candy Bar and I caught up with it in a cherry-red bumper car we had jacked from a phets dealer on Coney Island. He'd been slipping the Tsar some bad shit, and we used that as a pretense to cut him up and steal his stuff (we didn't cut him up too bad; he still had a few fingers left, I think, but Sisterhood gnawing at his balls really scared him). With the bumper car, which we had christened Sheila, we drove straight into the window of one of the old Kaiser Mart grocery stores and through the glass, which broke like fireworks spitting up all over us. We stocked up on breakfast cereal and soymilk, and those energy bars hikers like so much, and then stopped to admire the vista.

The Kaiser Mart had been closed for a year or so, since an armed robbery had gone awry there, and no one could bear to deal with the remains. The crime scene was as fresh (or as foul) as the day it happened. The bodies of the victims of stray bullets were sprawled at awkward angles halfway down the aisles. Mothers crouched over toddlers, old ladies with baskets full of cat food, homosexual couples with fingers interlaced, spinsters in piles of dusty *Vogue* magazines and, occasionally, a supermarket worker flat on his back, hand held out in pointless defense, face contorted in terror. The scenario had been preserved in pristine condition by the air conditioning, nothing had decayed, one little boy had hold of a teddy bear in a sweater that read *Aloysius*, and I adopted him.

The Kaiser Mart sound system still worked, and it played light R&B and jingles advertising special offers on frozen foods and dairy products. If I were a reflective person I would have called it eerie, but I wasn't, so I didn't. I didn't even find it terribly interesting; it was just one of those things. Sisterhood howled along with the Muzak and raced up and down the aisles, glad to stretch her legs.

"Wrong time, wrong place," said Candy Bar, surveying the splayed, petrified corpses and chewing on a licorice shoelace.

I admit that made me shudder. I looked over my shoulder, but Sisterhood appeared not to have noticed.

"Get in girl," said Candy Bar, and she started the engine. "Pompeii. Pompeii! That's what this place reminds me of, it was on the tip of my tongue. Pompeii. Have you ever been? It's sick."

I had heard that in Pompeii the walls were covered in ancient filth, the fuckings of antiquity, and that when it was rediscovered by some fruity Victorian grave robbers all females were banned from visiting the dirtiest bits. People always said that this was because women back then were too delicate to see that kind of terrible thing, but obviously it was because all those fruits wanted to get together and jerk off and lick the walls, the way all little boys do with stolen porno mags. I thought about telling Candy Bar my thoughts on the matter, but I knew she'd probably get uptight and go on and on about how I was a lesbian separatist (which I am). Driving always makes her agitated. Besides, we were late.

It only took us a day or so to catch up with the train—me, Candy Bar, Sisterhood and Aloysius. Travelling by bumper car, we had the advantage of not needing to refuel every three hours since our Dodgem ran on electricity, its great, big, flaccid stinging pole sparking away like a scorpion's tail above us. And besides, we didn't have the weight of a movie star's corpse slowing us down, so soon we were upon the train. We skimmed alongside, having no choice but to follow it since we didn't know where the funeral was being held. Behind us, a fleet of barefoot peasants plodded along with the same intention—Valentino was a man of the people. I imagined this is what it was like when Popes were buried or ordered their followers to head out East to slaughter Muslims, an unshod motley gathering. Candy Bar drove on, whistling Joni Mitchell's *Lesson in Survival*, whilst Sisterhood perched erect on all fours, sticking her head over the front windshield and panting, with her tongue hanging from her mouth in motorway excitement. Aloysius and I, bored, watched television on a portable set and ate Frosties.

We saw so much of the world, and it was fields of dead grass, suffocated crops, dry, broken river beds and stony soil ringing concentric circles around towns like outposts. All

107

along the northern horizon ran a wall, a slate fence beyond which it was said people lived; lived, that is, in the relative comforts of the old world. But that was just a conspiracy theory. All along the wall I read and reread the same phrase: "Resistance is Fertile," and thought to myself what a great tattoo that would make.

We were forced to make countless stops all through the day and night, as the train took in diesel and coal and its staff fell out into the bitter chill of New Mexico and sobbed. On one of these breaks from what was becoming a pretty relentless journey, I noticed that we were in Veronica Springs, a familiar town, and jolted awake.

"This is where my mother lives!" I yelled, and we all got out of the bumper car.

I found my mother at home, in sweat pants and a sport shirt emblazoned with a sunset and the slogan *Paradise Beach*, working out to a Jane Fonda videocassette issued shortly before the revolution. She wore a Snoopy headband and moved in total precision with the workout routine, so much so that I had to wonder if my mother were not in fact Jane Fonda. I'd never asked. She went on exercising for a good few minutes before she acknowledged the four of us.

"I wanted to wait until I was sure you were real," she explained, patting her brow with a towel, "before I said anything. It can be terribly embarrassing to find yourself talking to figments of your imagination, you know. Not to mention depressing when they don't answer back!"

She made tea for us all, and we caught up over a nice selection of finger sandwiches and delicate pastries. She said

I looked a little different and wanted to know what I'd been doing since I was born.

"Oh, this and that," I said and ate another fondant fancy.

"Well, you won't believe it," she said, "but Jackie, you know Jackie from the office, well, she had a hysterectomy last year and they discovered that she was actually one of two twins, and that her sister had been living in her womb for thirty-seven years. Isn't that incredible? I told her to give *Woman's Own* a call, because you can get fifty quid for a true-life story, if it's good enough. But she didn't want to. She said it was degrading to put yourself out there like that, and I said, 'What are you talking about Jackie? Public's the new private! Didn't the Prime Minister get voted in on the back of a TV talent contest? If it's good enough for Winston Churchill it's good enough for you, love!'"

Candy Bar had the hiccups.

"And I've lost so much weight, don't you think?" She twirled around the room. "Barbarella gave me some of this amazing diet powder; you just dissolve it in your seven-up and you don't even feel a little bit hungry! Gives you a terrible headache, though, and you do feel a bit edgy, but the weight just falls off. Well, you see Barbarella was getting the stuff, speed as it turned out to be, from this boyfriend of hers that was always beating her up. So when she killed him by dropping a toaster into the bathtub with him, well, I was high and dry. Or rather *not* high and dry! Ha! Ha! That's when I dug the Jane Fonda tapes out of the loft, they're illegal now you know, but they're very collectable, not that I'd ever sell them. Anyway, I started working out, just as a replacement for the whizz at first, but I found I really quite liked it. As it happened, this fella in a bright yellow sports car gave me a load of Ritalin just last week, which is just as good, and purer than street speed, anyway, and I let him stay here for a few nights when he was having the clutch replaced on his car."

With my mouth full of choux bun and my face all sticky with icing I asked:

"A yellow car? Was it a convertible?"

"Yeah," said my mother, "and there were these two old blind ladies with him, too, and their daughter Audrey, gorgeous baby she was. I think they'd had artificial insemination, you know, where they put the baby inside you, already baked? They might have, it's very popular with lesbians. Zhandra, who lived next door, was a lesbian, you know."

My mother went on to explain that in the past few years, besides (or maybe because of) becoming a speed freak she had also achieved a considerable level of success as the front woman for the post-punk riot girl band, Daisy Division. She showed us (unasked) video footage of herself onstage in a shredded *Haggy Bear* T-shirt and skintight stonewash jeans, screaming, spitting, kicking. I put my hand over Aloysius' eyes, Candy Bar was mesmerized.

"Do not even think about fucking my mother," I hissed at her through my teeth.

My mother punched the air and rocked out in her sweat suit as she cleared the table. "We're playing in D.C. soon," she said. "It's too bad you kids aren't sticking around, you should come and see us." She pinched my cheek and stroked my hair. "Or do you think you'd be embarrassed to see your old Ma kickin' it onstage?"

I was touched and felt the sadness of snowflakes melting. I wanted to reach out for her hand, but she had gone into the kitchen. How had I come to be her daughter? How had she forgotten me entirely, after my birth in a bowling alley, and abandoned me to the lusty caretaking of my putrid father? I would have liked to ask her, but it didn't seem polite when she had already gone to such effort with the tea and cakes. At exactly three–thirty, we heard the whistle blow for the train's departure, and Candy Bar insisted we get up to leave.

I kissed my mother goodbye. Gesturing to Sisterhood, she said, "Don't forget the dog's cadaver! She's stinkin' the place up, poor old girl. Lord, how your father loved that dog, the old fool!" She waved us off. "And don't forget to write!"

I took Sisterhood's liquefying corpse by her leash and dragged her to the bumper car. "Say goodbye, Aloysius," I said to Aloysius.

Candy Bar blew a kiss, and that was that—no more picket fences for me.

"Fucking train," I muttered. "Fucking Rudolph Valentino."

"Hey, don't knock Valentino, girl! Get in the car and wave to your mother."

I turned to look. My mother was on her porch smoking a cigarette and lifting weights, and we waved to each other.

"Did she put speed in our tea, do you think?" Candy Bar asked. "'Cos' I feel kinda anxious, you know, strung out."

"Candy, you always feel like that," I said. "It's your mode of operation."

"I guess."

Aloysius closed his eyes and sighed. It was naptime. He'd had a busy day, and I was very much relieved that he at least didn't shit himself like babies do. Sisterhood was silent. We followed the train on again as it pulled out of town, and I started to notice posters for my mother's band on nearly every street corner—a perfect example of how, once you realize something is there, you see it everywhere. Soon we were no longer stopping behind the train because the train was no longer stopping because the train had stopped, and we were in Los Angeles, which is where everybody goes to die or become immortal.

Twelve

The walk of fame was still there, although the brass plates had worn down. Eroded by so much panic-stricken foot traffic, so many sandstorms, such a lot of neglect, it was no longer possible to tell Lassie from Greta Garbo. The big talk was that all of the stars were to be reset in platinum (which was now entirely worthless but still beautiful, if that's possible) and that every plaque would be dedicated to Elizabeth Bathory, which I thought was a jolly good idea. What's the difference between a movie star and an aristocratic serial killer, anyway? Details, details.

All along the strip, celebrities impersonated themselves, wore Halloween-store replicas of their most iconic costumes and posed for pictures with the cyborg population (cyborgs *love* movie stars). Candy Bar and I were especially taken by the Mae West figure, who looked just like the real thing, which of course she was; so we asked for a picture and an autograph, which she kindly agreed to, on the condition that we leave Sisterhood with her. This seemed like a good deal; and Sisterhood, being both a dog and dead, did not seem averse to the idea, so we posed with Mae West and then left the stinking, maggot-riddled canine carcass at her feet. I asked her if she happened to know where Valentino was to be buried. Famously disinterested in questions not related to her own sex-bomb persona, Ms. West shook her head passive-aggressively and scowled, "What do I look like? The Citizen's Advice Bureau?"

I had to admit that she did not.

Departing, I heard Sisterhood clear the air by asking her what it was like working with Cary Grant. Casually I remembered a summer, several years ago, during which Sisterhood and I had watched *She Done Him Wrong* on a loop, while on a dope jag.

"Poor bitch," I sighed to myself.

Other than that, it was all drugstores, drugstores, drugstores for miles and miles and miles. Everything was now legal in Los Angeles—drugs, carjacking, child molestation, murder in all degrees, aggravated assault, assault with a deadly weapon, sexual assault, tax evasion, fraud, identity theft, breaking and entering, rape, circulation of indecent material, arson, kidnapping, false imprisonment, and euthanasia. The only currency was mescaline, and everyone tripped around the clock and committed crime after crime after crime, laughing wildly at the lizards (which were of course kindergarten teachers) they were stabbing through the face in the streets.

Infanticide was the sport of choice for wealthy Angelenos. It was de rigeur at social events of any standing and many socialites began to breed horses especially for such occasions (not to ride, of course, but for them to chew up the children). For more intimate affairs, blowing up abortion clinics was en vogue, and red-letter days suddenly had a whole new meaning. What could be more elegant than killing children who had already been killed? It was the perfect accompaniment to the refried beans served at the events by ladies in deathly chic black-satin frocks with giant bows in their hair, daubed in heavy black mascara and chaperoned by gentlemen in dinner jackets and diamond tiepins (the sartorial equivalent to a death's head on the lapel, don't you know?). Cocktail parties thrown to mark the release of a compendium of natural history trivia, or a collection of short stories, were held in the lobbies of the clinics themselves; and after a few martinis and a couple of speeches, the party-goers would toss grenades into operating theaters and counseling rooms and (just for good luck) behind the secretary's desk. Everybody would positively yelp (In delight? In horror? Who knows?) at the tidal waves of blood gushing through doorways, up the walls, and all over the linoleum floor tiles. Fleshy fireworks going off like a twenty-one-gun salute. *Bang-bang you're dead! Oh, and so are you and so are you and so am I!* Deviance is, of course, relative; and though it might seem outrageous, barbaric, bloody and unthinkable to you now, in the future it won't be—I promise.

Since everything was now legal, there were no more weekly televised executions of petty criminals. For a while, FOX had shown stock footage of pickpockets in the stocks having their eyes gouged out and re-runs of particularly notable hangings, such as the occasion in which one old man's head came entirely separated from his withered body during the fun, or the occasion in which it took one particularly pregnant lady twenty minutes to fully asphyxiate. (People complained about the hanging of a pregnant woman until the fetus was tried herself and found guilty as an accessory to murder.) Sadly, such vintage filth could not satiate the general public; and so, General Public, the military governor, agreed to reinstate live executions, this time using aspiring singer-songwriters and homeless gypsies (basically anyone who would do it for a grand) as the stars of the show. The phone lines were jammed every week, and the queues outside the last three working phone boxes in Wolverhampton stretched out for two days, as people dialed manically to place their vote to decide which contestant would go to the scaffold first.

Candy Bar had seen it all before.

The two of us revved up the bumper car and rode around trying to find something to wear to Valentino's funeral, which was taking place in the next day or so. We had been told to keep an eye on the cover of *Vanity Fair* for an announcement and planned to spend the intermediate time getting together just the right ensembles. We started out in a butcher shop where we picked up a great sinewy length of pig intestine for Candy Bar to wear as a boa. I myself selected a reddish brown lamb chop to wear as a hat, and we left, heading straight next door to Cartier for the jewelry. (L.A. is *such* a convenient city when it comes to these things.)

Maria Felix was smoking a menthol, wearing Capri pants and stroking a crocodile, screaming at the jeweler, who was slumped over the glass counter dead with a knife sticking out of his back. We said, "Good day," and helped ourselves to the stones and metals, prying open cabinets with a crowbar and delving into the sludge of jewels, a pick'n'mix for the world's most opulent, and now, for us.

"Darling," purred Candy Bar, "don't you think these opals will just look ravishing against my offal?"

"Divine!" I had to agree. It was a flawless match, and I picked up a handful myself.

"No, not for you," hollered Maria Felix. "Rubies for you." She slung me a string across the room, and I tried them against my hat, held them against my bleached bones. She was right, of course. How could I have ever doubted her?

For shoes, we rummaged around in trash cans; I pulled out the most marvelous pair of emerald-green slingbacks, and Candy found some perfectly serviceable army boots in a deep red; so she was shod in ox-blood, and I, in viridian. To test out our new *bottines* we strolled down an alleyway and kicked a sleeping tramp to death. All that was left for us to find were purses, and I knew just the place.

As a child I had always wanted to eat at fast-food restaurants, but my father had refused to take my brother and me on the grounds that it would be bad for our health. Even after Tom killed himself, I was still forbidden. Now I had the opportunity to prove my total independence; my rebuttal of the Electra complex would take place over a hamburger and fries in a little cardboard cartoon box, which I would then carry to the funeral of Rudolph Valentino as an evening bag.

"Very symbolic," Candy Bar nodded solemnly, and I realized that I had been talking aloud, and in a rather grandiose voice.

Thus attired, we were free to relax for the rest of our vacation. We chose to drive the bumper car to the outskirts of the city, where Candy Bar had remembered the red-light district was situated. We were both as horny as Hell (a place I always imagined to be full of sexual tension). As whores ourselves, we were entitled to a substantial discount from others of our kind, and we were sure to carry our customer loyalty card with us at all times. Candy Bar really just wanted to find someone we could bathe in champagne, and all I wanted to do was get naked and make out—and really, was that a lot to ask for?

We headed toward what seemed like the city limits; only we didn't find any prostitutes, just a group of small boys in the street devouring the remains of a dog. I guess they could have been prostitutes, but if that was the case, they weren't what we were looking for; I have always preferred the aftereffects of puberty. Candy Bar, too, and on that she was insistent.

Having passed the bloody little boys, we were soon in amongst an endless golden meadow, a field of dreams flourishing on a mass grave, the very last souvenir of the great war crimes committed during the revolution by the outgoing regime, or the incoming government, or the intermediary administration. Nobody could really say, despite the newspaper men being positive that five or twenty thousand people went missing, were mutilated and had their heads posted on spikes in a ring around the city.

Flora has a magnificent tendency to bloom at unprecedented rates upon great heaps of decomposing flesh. They say that in France, after the fabulous First World War, the land formerly known as No-Man's flourished as a vista of poppies, an opiate tribute to those who would never be forgotten, until they were. And then, after the sexy Second World War, all the concentration camps in Poland were entirely overtaken by bright yellow tulips, the seeds of which had blown in from Holland. I suppose it's something to do with all of that delicious nitrogen being released so richly in such high quantities and qualities into the soil to nourish the roots and bulbs of new blossoms. Flowers are greedy, hungry for your death.

We lay down to sleep (which is a lot like dying, only not as merciful) on the grass, between the skulls and the daffodils, with Aloysius squashed between us. The air was thick with dragonflies passing about us, an electric current on the breeze still hissing my name. We collected rocks for pillows and snoozed. With our heads together, Candy Bar's dreams leaked into mine and mine into hers and we ran through dark houses together, terrified, sleeping fitfully under the midday sun. In Los Angeles it is always midday, it is always too hot to think and everybody travels everywhere on roller skates, which makes daydreaming an impossibility. Little moths, *Acherontia Lachesis*, settled on us in great numbers, smothering our faces with their folded wings, forming a golden brown carpet over our barely breathing bodies. They departed before we awoke, and we dreamed on, undisturbed. We only know of this occurrence because we watched the replay later on CCTV when we took jobs as night watchmen at the mall.

The next morning, if it is to be believed that we slept through the night, we headed straight to the newsagent to peruse the appropriate magazine covers for news. There wasn't any.

Thirteen

It was quite clear that we were running out of time. We were on a quest, after all, or hadn't you noticed? We had a funeral to gatecrash, and more importantly, I was responsible for bringing the curtains down on the universe. (*It's really too bad*, I thought to myself, *that once I have destroyed all human life, there will be no one to sell my story to!* And I almost quit right there and then.) We believed that the only people who could furnish us with information were the Valeries, a girl gang of ruthless street killers dedicated to the destruction of the new world order. The Valeries knew everybody's business. Luckily, Candy Bar had an in with them, since her kid sister had been kidnapped and brainwashed by them and was now a high-ranking commandant. I thought to myself what a great idea that would have been for Baby; instead of ditching her with Thackeray and the Catholic missionaries, I could have handed her over to the Valeries, where she would have been put to good use and been assured protection from sexual abuse (well, mostly). But that had not been the case.

The Valeries had a secret hideout, of course, and the two-mile radius around the premises was patrolled by gang members swinging baseball bats. These bitches were tough, and they were all under ten years old.

120

"Oh yeah," said Candy Bar, "they're all just little girls, but they're the most feared gang in L.A. This is no custard gun, *Bugsy Malone* shit."

I didn't doubt it. In my brief and blood-splattered life, which weighed on me and my creaking hips like an eternity, I had seen (no, that's too reductionist; I had *experienced*) many troublesome things, but never really, until then, fear. Escorted inside the Valeries somewhat chintzy compound, which had been sunk underground by a sonic blast several years earlier, we were brought face to face with a church hall full of little girls in party dresses and pigtails, chewing gum and polishing assault rifles. Occasionally they would stop for a game of musical statues, which they played with maniacal glee, or take a break to groom their My Little Ponies; but for the most part they prepared, constantly, for turf war.

The church hall was laid with waxed-pine floorboards, and there was a big fat piano at the far end at which sat a big fat piano teacher, Mrs., Varney, who banged out *Pop Goes The Weasel, Zip-a-dee-doo-dah* and *When father Papered the Parlour* on an endless spinning round, at the end of which the children would all cheer and yell, "Once more Mrs. Varney, if you please."

Mrs. Varney was only too happy to oblige. Mrs. Varney was not an authority figure; no, the Valeries were nonhierarchical and took orders from no one, least of all a fifty-five-year-old pianist. They had all had mothers and fathers once, but it was part of a girl's initiation to kill her parents (and some had been as young as two when they did), so the Valeries had no first-hand experience of patriarchy, or matriarchy, for that matter. Untied, unmoored, unrestrained by family, sentimentality or, in fact, anything other than businesslike sisterhood, the Valeries were free to kill, maim and slaughter without fear of repercussions and dedicate each strike against the new world order to the honor of those little girls who had gone before them.

The Valeries were initially suspicious of us.

"That," a blond Valerie asked, pointing to me but speaking to Candy Bar, "is that a boy? Did you bring a boy to our undisclosed location?"

"No," she replied calmly. "That's La Diana, and she's totally a daughter of the moon."

It was time for jelly and ice cream. The Valeries all slung their assault rifles over their shoulders and formed an orderly line at a sagging paste table, pleasantly decorated with a plastic Cinderella tablecloth and serving as a buffet bar.

"Guests first," one of the Valeries insisted, shoving Candy Bar and I to the front of the line.

(They may have been a little rough, but the Valeries had impeccable manners.)

After dinner we were interrogated again. I gave extensive testimony on my rape, pregnancy, labor and long-term love affair with Candy Bar as proof that I was not the man, not a man, not even really human but certainly not a cyborg (everybody knows cyborgs are all child molesters, it's in their wiring).

"Well," announced one three-year old Valerie, "if she says she's not a man, she isn't a man. It's her prerogative to decide for herself. A woman's right to choose, right?"

Mrs. Varney punctuated the statement with a musical flourish. *Da-da-da-dah!*

Candy Bar asked, "Have you seen my sister Valerie anywhere? Is she still with you? Still operative? She was about four when she joined, so she must be about ten now. Has anybody seen her?"

A six-year old spoke up. "Oh, yeah, Valerie. She's on sentry duty in the 16th quadrant tonight; she gets off anytime now. More jelly?"

Candy Bar declined, opting to step onto the patio and light up her pipe. "Better for the children's health if I smoke out here," she acknowledged.

The Valeries started to discuss their aggressive takeover of Bank of America. The CEO of said corporation was being held hostage in one of the cells within the compound. They were going to kill him anyway, but if Bank of America agreed to sign itself wholly and completely over to them, they would only shoot him rather than perform the rather elaborate execution they had planned in case Bank of America refused.

Hanged, drawn and quartered was the traditional death of traitors until the 1960s, when treason was taken up by American presidents as a way to kill time during long weekends; hence it become *de trop*. Now the Valeries had decided to reinstate it. After they had gutted the French Minister of Finance and the head of Marketing at Coca-Cola (in the same week, no less, *quite* an achievement!) the process had become extremely fashionable amongst rebels, guerrillas and dissidents, which is to say, everyone; though no one could top the erotic power of the image of a cabinet minister being disemboweled by four little girls, each dressed as a Disney princess. The Valeries even graced the cover of *Vogue* in their replica regal regalia, under the headline *Top Ten Icons under 10*.

Not since the SS terrorized the populations of Eastern Europe had a uniform provoked such unbridled horror, hysteria and blind fear in the citizenry. The mere sight of Snow White in the street was enough to imbue a man with a shaking, suffocating, pants-shitting, vomit-inducing fit of uncensored terror. Luckily, the Valeries knew a good dry cleaner (which was obviously a money laundering front) who owed them a few favors; and so their costumes were always pristine, and they never swore—except for oaths. All considered they were perfect little angels.

At the meeting, there were charts, maps, slideshows, atlases, cutlasses and new weapons on display, as well as a debate on what to do with a rival gang—the Margarets. Once they had the funds from the Bank of America takeover, the Valeries would be totally invincible. They'd buy up all of Iran's plutonium for a start; in fact, they'd buy Iran. Having technology at their fingertips, their seizure of security contracts and the malice with which they would operate them would undeniably make them top dog. The Margarets would be sure to try and strike before the merger was finalized or face inevitable and total obliteration. The Valeries were thus on high alert. Admittedly, our arrival had been poorly timed.

Returning from the patio with a little bit of a suntan, Candy Bar tiptoed in and sat beside me.

"You should see the garden, it's full of flamingos, hundreds of pink flamingos."

I had often dreamt of flamingos, which in sleep symbolize the beginning of a new community, or conversely, an over-dependence on one's looks. Shortly after pushing out Baby, I had dreamt that I gave birth to a flamingo and then promptly devoured it, devouring my own good looks by proxy (*Eat Yourself* has always been my mantra.) I'd do very well as a cannibal, if only I weren't one of a kind. If you go killing other species it's merely murder, and that has been done to death. Briefly I thought back again to the walk of fame dedicated in its entirety to Elizabeth de Bathory. You have to admit she had style.

The Valeries decided that there was only one thing to do: blow up the monolithic diet corporation, Slim World, to show the Margarets that they weren't to be fucked with. They'd have us come along on the mission to prove our loyalty. They kitted us out with AK47s, lead us to the garage, into an armored four-by-four and out into the misty sunshine of that smog-thick city. It was almost beautiful.

The truck was monstrous, bouncing in the potholes of the unmaintained roads, chewing up all the parked cars and pedestrians in its path, and spitting out the bones of detractors and critics and uneducated naysayers. Inside, to get us in the mood, the Valeries played Death Metal, which is, personally, all the evidence I need to accept the fact that, yes, rap does drive impressionable young people to violent acts. The car was pristinely clean and smelt like the pine air freshener that hung from the rearview mirror. One of the Valeries stood on the backseat to man the flamethrower in the rear. Testing it, she took out a petrol station, the explosion of which decimated a significant portion of the surrounding residential area. Candy Bar had yet to see her sister.

We pulled up outside the Slimming World building, a pure glass stalagmite kissing the hazy low-lying atmosphere of late afternoon. This, then, was the target—kaboom. The Valeries marched in double file, armed to the teeth, slick, flawless, fierce and deadly; and it struck me that little girls and drag queens are ultimately the same thing, imitations of imitations, becoming wilder with each extrapolation.

In their satin ruffles and oversized bows, gingham dresses and patent shoes, they burst into the foyer of the conglomeration and filled it full of lead; the receptionists barely had time to scream for mercy. Making their way directly to the third floor, with a cry of "God Bless Lily St. Cyr" the Valeries liberated all the middle-aged ladies chained to exercise bikes whose constant workouts provided the whole tower with power; and the building blacked out. The women ran shrieking with joy out of the building back to their wives and families, who were all now obviously dead, killed by the persistent wars, plagues, revolutions and mass murders that defined the era.

In total darkness, we made our way up the stairs to the sixty-sixth floor, where we found the President of Slim World yelling to his bodyguards in a fit of panic upon hearing the tap-tap-tap of twenty murderous little girls coming his way, the way one hears the soft swoopings of the wings of Azrael and screams.

"You bitches wouldn't dare," he barked, lit only by a flashlight and looking like a fleshy, waxy, melting pumpkin.

The Valeries cocked their revolvers.

"Fuck you, you little bitches, you pack of fucking little cunts."

The Valeries disliked profanity and looked upon eloquence as one of the highest virtues. It was obvious that the President of Slimming World was not making much headway with them.

"You are a fascist pig," said one of the Valeries. She was eight or nine and had a suitable air of authority about her. "And we intend to show you what we do to fascist pigs."

The Valeries dragged one of the President's bodyguards across the room. Kicking and screaming, he pissed his pants bright yellow. The Valeries shot off his kneecaps and slung him like a pig's carcass over the President's desk. When he regained consciousness he wished he hadn't, for his pants were around his ankles, resting on his Italian lace-ups, and the Valeries were wedging an un-lubed revolver into his asshole. He looked up, suddenly alert, at the President's horror-stricken face, a seven-year-old Valerie pulled the trigger and his intestines splattered like action painting out through his mouth and across the President's face, like an ejaculation. The smell was terrible.

"*That* is what we do with fascist pigs, Mr. President."

The President of Slimming World was slack-jawed with shock. He tried to form sentences but merely stammered. *Moments of great trauma, moments of great trauma, moments of great trauma*, I whispered to myself.

"We know for a fact that you are in cahoots with the Margarets, which directly contravenes our previous advice to you, and that is a very ungrateful way to behave. That alone is enough for us to castrate you, tie you to an office chair and push you out of the window, without even referencing the fact that you are antifeminist and a corporate blood-sucker who feasts on the very people you claim to help, jacking them up on speed and letting them hope that they can modify their bodies to fit your deplorable fantasies."

"Big is beautiful!" came the chorus, and then the Valeries left the room, left the President shaking and screaming, out of his mind with the grotesquerie of the situation.

They left him with a handgun gift-wrapped expertly by Candy Bar with a tag that read, "Use Me." As we trailed out double file back to the foyer, we heard a single shot. The President had killed himself. For most people that would be enough, but the Valeries were not (in case it has eluded you) most people, and so they blew the entire building up with an innovative mixture of dynamite and *démaquillant*.

Big, gooey raindrops fell from the building as the blast tore it apart, setting alight everything they touched. We watched the disaster from under the mournful safety of Winnie the Pooh umbrellas. The tower collapsed under it's own weight, and I felt a touch saddened by an ironic melancholy for Alfred the Chemist, who had established the Nobel Peace Prize. In the ruins of the building, we sieved for valuables that would become reliquaries and souvenirs. On the evening news, the attack was reviewed sympathetically (the Valeries had twisted the arm of the broadcasters very high behind their back). The atrocity was reported, simply, as a tragedy, under the headline, "Plane hits tower."

Thirteen

"Girl," croaked Candy Bar, "I have the worst hangover ever. *Seriously*, what were we mixing with that Tequila?"

"Everything," I whimpered, and then threw up over the side of the boat.

To celebrate the destruction of Slim World, their takeover of Bank of America and the complete annihilation of the Margarets, the Valeries had thrown an enormous shindig on their yacht, *HMS Revenge*. She was a stately vessel that had once belonged to the Queen of England, who owed the Valeries a few favors and finally handed it over one Christmas after a particularly unlucky streak in a gin rummy tournament. The Valeries, however, still thought very highly of Her Majesty and neither mocked nor tortured nor killed her upon their victory. Indeed, they still sent the old girl a birthday card every year, and in return the Queen had made them all Duchesses. The Valeries had casks upon casks of rum, tequila and other pirate spirits onboard, so much so that the yacht bobbed uneasily on the surface of the water at the dock, almost going under.

I remember very little… flashes of strobe lights, karaoke singing, Mrs. Varney passing out up on the deck in a mammoth pool of puke, streamers fluttering wildly in the breeze of dawn. Having finally found her sister, Candy Bar had disappeared under the mahogany buffet table for a heart-to-heart bonding session. She was gone for over an hour before surfacing with mascara smeared around her eyes, confused in the realization that she had been mistaken; the girl was not her sister. We drank more, a lot more, and got tattoos from two filthy sailors who engraved our biceps in the excruciating Japanese style, adorning us with the Valeries' motto, *Mother May I?*, encircled in flowers in bloom. We were now officially affiliated with the Valeries. If anyone should ever fuck with us, one glimpse of our tattoos would be enough to stop them in their nefarious tracks, if it didn't gorgonize them entirely.

Candy Bar and I had also gone blond, peroxiding our hair in one of the yacht's luxuriously upholstered bathrooms, and also bleaching out parts of the woodwork, staining the carpet and leaving smudged handprints on the faucets and mirrors. We looked more alike now than ever, like a pair of ladies from Shanghai lying flat on our backs on that ocean liner, woozy and seductive. We knew it was time to go.

"Nothing lasts forever," said Candy Bar, misty-eyed. "There's a car park in Berlin where Hitler's bunker used to be, you know?"

I did know.

"We should visit," she continued.

The Valeries, normally stoic to the point of almost being uptight, waved us off the boat with genuine emotion. Some of the very little ones started to cry and had to be soothed with pacifiers by the older Valeries. Mrs. Varney gave us an upbeat but undeniably teary rendition of *There'll Be Bluebirds Over*

The White Cliffs of Dover as we disembarked, heading ashore for the ever-delayed funeral of Rudolph Valentino.

The Valeries were sorry that they had been unable to give us any useful information as to where Valentino's funeral would be held (which was really very gracious, especially as we had entirely forgotten to ask them about it, caught up in the revelry and the terrorism as were we). It just goes to show exactly how much of everything the Valeries knew about. They told us that upon disembarking from the ship we would be entering dangerous territory and gave us cat masks from the Halloween store to wear so that we could go undetected as we attempted to find the funeral service. Trusting the Valeries, who seemed unquestionably right so far, we walked down the gangplank to the dock, a tad sorrowful, even with the sunlight streaming into our eyes, the Valeries throwing a shower of confetti about our shoulders, and Mrs. Varney's piano (badly in need of tuning) playing at our backs.

All along the marina, little houseboats sat like ducks on a pond, big wooden ducks that couldn't fly or move independently, ducks that didn't respire, reproduce or excrete (once you investigate a metaphor, you often find it doesn't work).

Wearing the cat masks, we made our way to Paddington Station to collect our suitcases from the locker room, where we had sent them ahead of our arrival under the watchful eye of our porter, Aloysius. Candy Bar liked Paddington Station. She said it always made her feel like she was *really* going somewhere (Candy Bar can be so old-fashioned sometimes). That part of town was entirely populated by former fashion models. Indeed the area around Paddington Station had been declared an independent principality. Since no one was buying clothes, because all the fashion houses had fled to Vichy with the rest of the collaborators and advertising was banned, fashion models were now entirely useless. Some of them had successfully integrated with the cyborg population and hardly noticed the difference, so used were they to an entirely inhuman way of living; but many had become radical anarchists and set up their own community.

It's too bad that we lived in a world where dissent was as expected and necessary as death and taxes; except, of course, no one paid taxes to our nonexistent government. To want anything other than total destruction—now, *that* would have been radical. To walk amongst them, we *had* to wear our cat masks. We didn't want our faces to be seen, and in the costume cat masks we were invisible; we didn't want to be signed by an agency. As Candy Bar had put it, "Those who can't, model, right?"

At the station, now staffed by former models, all of whom were dressed in a solid-black uniform of jackboots, trench coats and berets, we were startled at the bizarre homogeneity of the scene. They all looked like the old Parisian Existentialists or the Black Panthers; I couldn't quite put my finger on which. The billboards all over the station had been defaced. Advertisements for beauty creams that had once read, *Your Face Is Your Fortune—Invest,* now declared in censored, wide-spaced language, *Face Your Fortune,* which I thought was, like, totally right on.

The roof of the train station was a swimming pool; and when they were not on patrol, the citizens and residents of the

Independent Principality of the Area Immediately Surrounding Paddington (terrible name, I always thought) swam there, long-legged and amphibious. The beautiful, like the rich, are at home anyplace, so they say, which of course means by extension that they are at home nowhere—that's why they stick together. They don't want their good looks to be squandered on bad genetic matches, or their fortunes to be wasted on the undeserving poor; and frankly, I don't blame them; but then, you see, that's because I am one of them, because I am an outsider, too. I don't belong, I am not at home, I must go on marching, searching for my impossible kind. By default I am rich and beautiful, too (for what it's worth), because the sum total of my life and their life is the same (zero); and if we work backward, we find that our input is equal. I am wealthy and gorgeous, too, and lonely, a soap-opera cliché.

They all had identical swimsuits, black of course, and they swam as though it were a religion, which it was. It was the only spiritual event left to a race entirely stripped of humanity in the name of profit, who'd been left to stand alone in their own glorious ruins when the bottom had fallen out of it all. This was not Hockney's California, and it weren't no country club, neither. Once or twice, clean out of nowhere, from a bright-blue crystal sky, lightning struck the water revealing the skeletons beneath the skin. Nobody died, and merely electrified, they swam on. The pool froze in winter (which never came, so why worry?), encasing the swimmers in sheets of ice, mammoths suspended for a season or so to thaw when the temperatures rose and revealed to future generations the story of what had come before them. In the summer, the water evaporated into steam and was lost, and the swimmers lay on their backs on the hot tiles at the bottom of the pool, staring at the sun, gasping like fish torn from the sea.

We opened our locker; mercifully, Aloysius was still there, keeping watch over our pitiful belongings and our exquisite funereal ensembles—thank goodness for teddy bears! Though the Valeries, Mae West, the popular press and the leaves at the bottom of my mother's tea cup had all proved useless in helping us discover where Valentino's funeral would be held (and, in truth, we had begun to feel rather worn out by the whole endeavor), Aloysius, little darling that he was, was sitting there, clutching our invite! It was printed in gold in a gothic font, revealing a service time less than an hour in the future, and hand-signed by Ms. Sisterhood G. Woof, Executive Assistant to the Cadaver of Signor Valentino. (I guess Mae West must have suggested her for the job).

We hurriedly dressed in a bathroom stall while I concurrently thought to myself, *Moments of great trauma,* and, *Ah! Just like the old days!* I helped Candy Bar into her backless evening gown of crushed velvet in deepest black, and she zipped me into my corseted black-satin knee-skimmer. We wrapped ourselves in the million-dollar jewelry and draped the admittedly stinking offal over our shoulders, squeezed into our ill-fitting shoes, and were ready. Aloysius had pressed his monogrammed sweater especially for the occasion and wore a little dicky bow, too, just for kicks. We really did look quite the triptych, made such a scene exiting the bathroom, could already feel the flash bulbs popping all over us, and the metallic taste of fame embittered my tongue and poured mercurial down my throat.

Part Three:
Too Far Gone

Thirteen

The funeral was taking place in Westminster Cathedral, just a short cab ride from Paddington Station. It was almost as though we had thought ahead. Valentino lay in state in front of endless rows of dignitaries, monarchs, admirals, presidents, movie stars, mime artists and bishops.

Naturally, everybody was wearing Bob Mackie, the exact same dress in fact. (Well, how else do you coordinate that many famous wardrobes other than to ensure that *everybody* wears the same thing as Princess Margaret, so as not to cause embarrassment?) The scene was a sea of bronze tassels and gold bugle beads convulsing softly with emotion as the Archbishop (wearing the identical dress himself) orated beautifully on the life and times of Rudolph Valentino.

A ripple of quiet distaste passed through the crowds when they saw what we were wearing. Aloysius and I apologetically squeezed in at the back, alongside a reporter from *Entertainment Tonight*—not only were we dressed inappropriately, we were late.

In spite of our tardiness, Candy Bar made her way straight to the casket and began a ruthlessly efficient, and dare I say *fabulous*, makeover of Valentino's celebrated visage. She buffed him up, glossed him, glittered him, drew on his eyebrows because they were too thin and disguised his slightly asymmetric chin. She powdered him lightly with lavender dust and cocaine; and only when she was satisfied that he looked gorgeous enough, did she return down the aisle to squash into the pew next to Aloysius and I. She did this rather noisily, her heavy footfall in her army boots disrupting the service profoundly and causing the congregation to turn en masse from the Archbishop's proselytizing and flash us a stare as one angry mob.

As if that wasn't enough, the telephone rang. Its long, shrill tones bounced around the Cathedral, echoing off the ancient stone walls, screeching long, thin, tinny notes like the off-key warbling of a no-hope soprano with delusions of operatic grandeur. The entire congregation bubbled with resentment, and the relentless ringing caused the Archbishop to stop the sermon midsentence and yelp, "Would somebody *please* answer that telephone?"

The instrument of our awkward circumstance was a big, old-fashioned thing, clumsy and wall-mounted, with a cordless receiver resting in its cradle. Being that Liza Minnelli was the closest to the telephone, she reached out and answered it with panache (obviously).

"Hello? Huh? Oh, sure, I'll ask, hang on a moment, would ya?" She scanned the crowd of outraged mourners and, with one hand cupped against the side of her mouth, hollered, "Is there a Diana here? A Di-a-na? There's a phone call for you, Diana, if you're here, dear."

Would that the ground could have chewed me up. I raised my hand timidly, blushing beetroot red.

"Scarlet for yeh!" I heard the tea lady in the row behind me exclaim.

Liza Minnelli spoke into the receiver, "Just a minute, caller, she'll be right with you." Resting her hand on the mouthpiece to mute her voice, she said, "Diana, baby, it's for you—she says it's important." The receiver was passed hand-to-hand, down and across the Cathedral, making its way to me in a most pronouncedly passive-aggressive manner. When finally it was thrust into my hand, I was so embarrassed I could barely raise my voice to speak.

"Yes," my voice cracked. I coughed to clear my throat. "Hello, this is Diana."

Well he-llo Diana! You are live on Tropicalia FM this morning, and we are broadcasting to an estimated number of people! Are you excited? Grrrr-eat! Now, you are the lucky girl who has been chosen at random by our computer to take the Tropicalia FM daily challenge—live on the air! Are you game? There's a star prize at stake, Diana, if you win! That's right. If you're successful you could be taking home this spectacular 320-piece hand-painted fully dishwasher-safe Elizabethan dinner service—a prize worth winning if ever there was one! Diana, all you have to do to get your hands on this beautifully unique porcelain set is bring about the end of the world, simple as that. So, Diana, tell us—are you ready to play? Do you have what it takes to be America's Next Top Exterminating Angel?

Blushing, I whispered into the receiver, "Look, now is really not a good time for me. I'll do what I can, okay?"

There was a click and the line went dead. I lowered the phone. There was silence.

"Quite finished there, have we?" asked the Archbishop.

"Well, I thought she was really terrific," chimed in Liza. "Terrific! But of course, she always is, I've seen every one of her West End shows, marvelous, just marvelous!"

"Miss Minooli, please!" said the frustrated Archbishop.

"It's Minnelli," she replied tartly.

"My apologies, Miss Minnelli—but please, could we get on with business now? Some of us have a celebrity mini-golf tournament to attend at three!"

Liza hung up the receiver, order returned (briefly) and the Archbishop continued his sermon. He serenely regaled the dearly beloveds with morals drawn from the life of Valentino, the highs and lows, the ups and downs, the swings and roundabouts, the this, the that, the other. I had seen Valentino's biography on the History Channel recently, so I found the whole thing rather boring. I was only there to support Candy Bar, who hadn't yet revealed to me that she was Valentino's illegitimate daughter (but I had guessed anyway). This was her hour of need. I wondered if it would be terribly rude to etch the scene before me into the wood on the pew in front of me. The look on the face of the woman from *Entertainment Tonight* told me it would, and I half wished that I was back at Paddington Station swimming with the models—heck I was even ready to take off my cat mask.

The service went on, and nothing more of note occurred

until I spied out of the corner of my eye the sinewy frame of Eartha Kitt, tiptoeing across the chancel and right up to the tabernacle where she poured a great big jug of LSD into the bejeweled chalice. I sniggered to myself, and to my left, Candy Bar threw me a look of pure shade, while to my right, the woman from *Entertainment Tonight* elbowed me sharply in the abdomen. It was then, doubled over in pain, straightening up and refocusing my watering eyes, that I saw a sight for which I was unprepared—Charlie Chaplin sitting in the front row next to Thackeray, who was sitting next to the Catholic missionaries, who were sitting alongside Baby, who was now five or six years old; and all of them were in Bob Mackie gowns. And they say this kind of thing only happens in the movies!

At some point—I don't know when because I was too busy pantomiming to Candy Bar the events of my past (Church being the only appropriate place for charades and confessions) and trying to discretely point out the who's who in the front row—the chalice was passed around and Eisenhower took the first sip. Coincidentally, and in a manner strikingly similar to that in which Christ turned water into wine and made the loaves and fishes feed the five thousand, the chalice full of holy wine (and LSD) circulated the whole motley congregation twice before it was empty, by which time Eisenhower was rolling on the floor.

Duchesses were all agog at the melting walls, newsmen started to fellate their microphones, politicians convinced themselves they were lizards and a couple of television actors stood up and yelled, back and forth to each other, "Sneakers!"

"Spaghetti!"

The whole place became a blasphemy against the moral values of a bankrupt society. I watched the mourners rip the dresses off themselves and others, as Baby played *Don't Dream It, Be It* on the grand organ above our heads (*Rocky Horror* always was her favorite picture). Since I knew what had happened, I had the upper hand and chose to be entirely objective, utterly neutral in my observations of the chaos, which I charted in a notepad (which was in actual fact the stone floor) as though I were Pliny the Elder. I might have convinced myself that I were Pliny the Elder—I might have actually *been* Pliny the Elder—had I not spotted him sitting in the third row next to Admiral Duncan, with whom he was naturally engaging in fornication.

Such wild sexual behaviors swept over the crowd that the foundations of the Cathedral themselves started to groan orgasmically and all the doves in the rafters swooped down on us in glorious Technicolor. The lady from *Entertainment Tonight* was deep in the process of gorging on Candy Bar's pussy when she signaled to me that the statue of Saint Sebastian in the vestibule had come to life. Then she fainted; and she wasn't even Catholic, so you can imagine.

Saint Sebastian made his way to me through the pools of writhing lovers and manic onanists and took my hand and guided it to his arrow wounds. I wrapped my fingers around the shaft of an arrow that was penetrating his chest just above the heart and I pulled hard, wrenching it out of his torso as he moaned. Then I set about yanking out the arrow through his shoulder and the arrows in his legs, the arrow through his stomach and the arrows through his arms. Miraculously (well, he was a saint), no arrow had damaged his beautiful face, though some might say that is more the work of homosexual icon painters than divine intervention.

I stroked his saintly chest, I brushed my fingertips on his lesions, I slipped my digits into those gashes and finger-fucked his wounds. Saint Sebastian's cries of pleasure grew louder, his cock grew harder, his eyes fluttered wilder, until he was entirely overcome with desire, flaming like the Holy Spirit above his head; and he whispered into my ear, "Fuck me." We fell on each other, two carnivorous beings, transcendental in our desire to devour; and under a rainbow brought about by sunlight falling through stained glass and diffracting through the mist of holy water in the air, we made love.

All around us, as though we were an island in a sea of islands, separate landmasses connected in attitude, as though we were Japan, mourners fucked in wildly incongruous pairs. Chancellors of the Exchequer squirmed under the crotches of Archdukes, and aged spinster Princesses fisted each other. Water sports and scat play soon made the whole Cathedral stink like the holy manger, and angels of light hovered, even holding candles above the heads of the few who were timid, lighting their way. The Archbishop wept openly, thinking this must surely be Paradise; and the Mexican Minister of Culture assured him it was, then came all over his shoes. Babies were conceived, born and grew up amongst all this. The lovers went on rolling and fucking and seducing their children and birthing their own grandchildren for decades, as Saint Sebastian and I tried endlessly to quench each other's lust, barely able to imagine what would happen if we were to cum.

The Cathedral floor was carpeted in all those discarded Bob Mackie dresses, adorned with a splendid array of underwear and jewelry, wigs, prosthetic limbs, pocket knives, revolvers, hand grenades, notepads, dentures, city guides, tubes of Chanel lipstick, umbrellas, coin purses, credit cards, tampons, tinned goods, ice cube trays, brandy bottles, suicide notes and memos for the babysitter. Truly, it looked as though the place had suffered a direct hit from above by a blitzkrieg bomb, which had somehow managed to pass through the roof without damaging it before detonating and blowing the inhabitants to pieces. Above it all, on the altar, stood Eartha Kitt with her super-eight camera, swinging it round, sweeping in cinematically for the best shots—whatever would Ladybird Johnson have to say about *this*? I raised my hands to her in thanks as Saint Sebastian slipped inside of me, and she blew me a kiss; then it started to rain cherry blossoms, and I knew it would all be over soon. I was twenty-seven, and Saturn had returned.

A lot of cigarettes were smoked as people sobered up; a lot of pizza was ordered. The Archbishop looked a little concerned about the mess, but happy nonetheless. Great big puddles of pre-cum and cum and mysterious, glistening secretions sparkled throughout the Cathedral, twinkled in the starlight of midnight—yes, it really was that late. Poor old Valentino had still not been buried, though a few considerate souls had taken it upon themselves to lift him out of his coffin so that he could be part of the orgy (after all, it was in his honor). His corpse was placed on the floor in front of the altar, whereupon some eagle-eyed admirer noted that the cadaver sported an erection, unzipped his fly and sat on it. Needless to say, not a lot remained of Rudolph Valentino's body once the festivities had subsided. The little that did survive (a glass eye, a few gold teeth and his spine) was quickly cremated and the ashes launched into outer space, as requested.

As for Saint Sebastian, I couldn't say. He left or disappeared or ascended—I didn't mind. Candy Bar asked me if I thought I was pregnant again, but I was pretty sure that I wasn't. My womb had healed over after I dated the omniscient Oracle, whom I was sure was getting a *big* kick out of this scene, the pervert.

Thirteen

Outside, under a rainbow suspended between two flying unicorns, Charlie Chaplin held up a dialogue card saying, "I was stupid to have left you, I'm sorry."

"Too right, Jack," I said, dragging hard on the last of Candy Bar's post-coital cigarettes.

Baby was talking to Aloysius on a grassy knoll under the crisp winter sky. They looked just like twins, and I was pleased they were getting along so well. Candy Bar was thrilling the Catholic missionaries with some sordid story of the first time she fucked her father (clearly fictitious since her father was an outright homo), Thackeray was somewhere around, and this is what we call resolution. The moonflowers on the side of the hill opened up slowly, like aroused assholes, and I thought of Saint Sebastian with a sigh – how romantic it all had been. It was, of course, all over the news.

The air fairly crackled with frost. My breath hung there like a thought unspoken, becoming simultaneously less relevant and more pressing, then vaporizing. The little lake outside the Cathedral had frozen over, but only with thin ice, the deadly kind that lured you in, like Narcissus, to your own grave.

I have always said that Narcissus got a bad rap. He was

set up. Yes, he excessively admired himself (I mean, don't we all? If we don't, who will?), but that was no reason to drown the poor bastard. Everybody knows that what he was really punished for was his utter lack of interest, sexual interest, in other people, which I think says far more about his murderers than it does about him, don't you?

He didn't want to fuck nymphs or stalkers. He just wanted to be left alone to jerk off to the video clips he made of himself jerking off over pictures he took of himself jerking off. He ignored his admirers for the sake of his own precarious mental health, or he sent them a dagger with a note that read, *Take a hint*, and folks got all uppity about it. Some people just cannot stand the idea that their sexual magnetism, which is to say, their self-worth, is as worthless as the therapist's couch it is hammered out on; so they bumped Narcissus off. Unfortunately for his killers, since we always want what we can't have (and everybody wanted Narcissus), he lived on after his death; and now, generations of art historians, ladies of a certain age, poetically repressed vicars, soft-core pornographers and fey teenage boys all pine over him collectively.

We were going home.

Polite as she was, at first Candy Bar was not deeply desirous of shacking up with my former lovers, my former daughter and my former compatriots in the psychosis on wheels that was Thackeray's car. I think she feared she'd lose me, she so liked to imagine that she had found me; but in truth, I was still lost, will always be lost. And anyway, since we had all been thrown back together so conveniently, and in such a neat and glorious scenario, I didn't think I had any right to turn down the invitation to step back into the banana-yellow convertible, overloaded as it was. Didn't I feel a little sentimental about the old jalopy? Just a touch of Vaseline on the rose-tinted lens? Was I warm with an ache to slide inside, step back in and roll on? Maybe.

Since our suitcases were packed (as always), our grievances forgotten (or at least overlooked) and Valentino was buried (sort of), there was no reason for us not to go home. "We could all do with a nice cup of tea," said Mercy.

"Amen to that," replied Charity.

There was just one more task at hand, ending the world; but Thackeray wondered if we wouldn't mind rescuing his mother, Myra, first. She was being held hostage in a Tudor manor house by her sister, Thackeray's auntie Tyra. It wasn't a terribly long drive to the manor, though it was a considerable squeeze to get us all into the convertible. After some initial fumbling, we popped the trunk open and made a little playpen for Baby and Aloysius there in the back, being careful not to exceed 97 km/h lest they fall out into the road if we hit a speed bump. Charlie Chaplin (whose advances I was tactfully trying to avoid) and the Catholic missionaries sat in the back gossiping wildly—well, as wildly as a silent movie star and two blind old ladies can gossip. In the front seat, alongside a permanently jellied Thackeray, I had a powerful feeling of déjà vu; and I can't say it thrilled me. Candy Bar shared my seat and held my hand.

The missionaries prattled on. "I swear, when we got caught up in that riot between the Peronistas and the Catholic Student League, I thought we would never get out alive! On the one hand I was blessing myself in the name of the Father, the Son and the Holy Ghost; and on the other, I couldn't help yelling 'Viva Evita!'—it was all so darn topsy-turvy."

Charlie Chaplin held up a sign that read, "She looked too fierce, ALWAYS. Dior for *days* and those furs were killing me, Miss thing. Mink in ninety-degree heat? Work!"

The missionaries nodded. Mercy (the shorter of the pair) picked up the conversation.

"You know, I liked Argentina, I really did, and Miss Evita really was something, everything like they said she was. She outdid Jackie O. as far as I'm concerned, and you know what they say about her! They say that she spent so much money on her couture that the White House expenses had to be disguised as military expenditure. Imagine: Miss Jackie fitted up like a nuclear war head, in a Chanel two-piece lined with hand grenades and an Hermès head scarf peppered with anthrax, dressed to kill girl, dressed to kill."

"But still," said Charity (the taller of the two), "Miss Evita would cut her down with just a *look*. She would read her before she could even open her mouth to speak. Bring them together at *any* ball and just you see if Miss Jackie wouldn't get chopped and Miss Evita get tens all round."

"Oooh, shady!" said Mercy. "Miss Jackie would kill a bitch just with the cut of her New Look gown, she would wipe Miss Evita right off that floor."

Charlie Chaplin held up signs reading "Work!" and "Fierce!" and "Bitch, Please!" at regular intermissions; but I myself zoned out entirely since, in my humble opinion (which no one ever asked and that's why I ran away from this goddam house!), both E.P. and J.K.O. paled in comparison to Snow White's stepmother when it came to competing in the category of Ultimate Legendary Sickest Wife of a Dictator Realness.

We pulled over at a gas station—it's always a gas station—and a very leggy blond drag queen with huge glittery lips came out the office to speak to the children in the trunk. She looked terribly maternal, and I wondered if she wouldn't like to come along with us as a live-in babysitter. She patted Aloysius on the head and asked Baby what her name was.

"Baby," Baby replied.

"Fabulous," said the drag queen and flipped her mane of immaculate curls over her shoulder. "Do you want gas?" she asked Thackeray.

"Oh sure, I mean that's why we're here, isn't it? Is it? Where exactly are we? Exactly?"

"This is Mexico City, and I'm its biggest star. You are currently on the forecourt of the Teatro La Blanquita petrol station and music hall. With every liter of petroleum you get a free admission to the floor show."

It was a very undistinguished gas station, slate gray, flat, moribund, undead, in that corseted, powdered-white-face, gothic, adult-erotica kind of way.

"Well," Thackeray said, "However many there are of us, give us that many liters of gas and we'll all be glad to see your production."

"Oh, it's more than a production," said the drag queen. "It's the future."

"Sure," I said, "the future, I've met her before."

The blond drag queen filled up our tank with gas. We idled on the forecourt, counting clouds in the pebble-dashed sky. A squelching sound approached the car from behind, a thumping, crawling rhythm punctuated with guffaws and causing the convertible to vibrate a little. The enormous, idiotic snail I had once encountered in the middle of the night in the middle of the desert dragged itself up to the car door.

"Hellowie!" it boomed and chuckled.

"Oh, hi there," I said, politely refraining from rolling my eyes too much, "nice to see you, again."

"Do..." the snail attempted, before breaking out into a fit of giggles, "do you...do you get it?" And here, the snail laughed uproariously, emitting a great, oozing puddle of slime about itself. "Do you get it now?"

Candy Bar, feeling defensive and protective, asked, "Diana, who is this?"

"Meeeee?" said the snail, suddenly serious. "I'm Berale, but you can call me Beryl!" and broke out in cacophonous laughter once again.

"Oh, brother," I sighed to myself, praying that this interaction wouldn't last much longer. "What's so funny?" I asked. "Why are you always laughing to yourself? It's so annoying! Are you high?"

Beryl ignored me. "Guess what?" the snail chuckled slyly.

"What?" I snapped

"I know something... I know.... I know something you don't know!" The goofy gastropod literally spasmed with hilarity, spraying us with a fine mist of spit.

"Can we go in now?" I asked the blond drag queen as she finished filling the tank.

"No," she replied, wiping a chunk of snail snot from her forehead. "Not yet. The show won't start for a little while." And she disappeared inside.

"Tee-hee-hee!" gurgled the snail. "Aren't you curious? Because I know someone who is curious about you!"

"Oh, just come out with it already!" barked Mercy.

"You heard the lady," seconded Charity, and Beryl the snail looked somewhat taken aback, put off stride.

The snail gestured with one eyestalk to Thackery. "*His* mother! Oooh yes, she's waiting for you! Nasty Knickers! She wants to give you, ooh-ha-ha! She wants to give you a big BANG! Wait till she shows you those knick-… those knick-… those KNICKERS!"

Thackery, oversensitive at the best of times, leapt up and lunged at the snail, fists clenched, and yelling, "How dare you? The woman is a saint! How dare you! I'll kill you."

The snail merely swung its gigantic head at Thackery and knocked him into the air with such force that he was thrown the length of the forecourt and landed, dazed, in a stack of tires. His comical expression as he tried to stand back up caused the snail to titter to itself and mumble, "It's going to be very special, oh yes, *very special*!" Here the titters became undulating belly laughs. "Nasty knickers and a big bang!" the snail howled out with laughter, smashing its head on the ground, overwhelmed with mirth and repeating, "a big bang! Ha! A BIG BANG!"

The blond drag queen reappeared in a dress made of lettuce leaves and told us we could begin to filter into the theater for the floorshow. As we filed in, she spoke to the snail with a tone of knowing familiarity. "Oh Beryl, you are going to have to stop this, love, you're really getting a name for yourself, you know." She straightened her wig. "Do you have a fag? Thanks. Now don't nibble on me dress. I've got a show to do in five minutes."

We went inside. Thackeray was terribly worried that the show would be of the sort that Mexico City was famous for, the sort he had read about extensively whilst a student of human intersexuality at Harvard, the sort of show that simply consisted of nine-year-old boys pulling down their underwear and bending over to show off and finger their prepubescent assholes. He got feverish at the thought, and I thought he might faint. He didn't, and we took our seats. Another queen, wearing nothing but a floor-length red wig, coyly draped to conceal her immodesty, sailed down the aisles selling popcorn and licorice. Baby pointed out, "In Farsi, 'popcorn' translates as 'elephant shit.'" (Baby is so well read.)

The show began; and much to my surprise, though nothing really surprises me anymore, it was a production of *Calamity Jane* with a full cast of female impersonators performing every role. We laughed, we cried; and when it came to the point Jane sings *Secret Love*, well, the whole audience sang along practically word for word. The magic of showbiz! The production transpired to be a double bill (the shows separated by a fifteen-minute instructional video on how to make the perfect pancake), and *Calamity Jane* was followed promptly by a version of Puccini's *Tosca*, which brought the house down, although, thankfully, not literally this time.

Candy Bar was astounded, the Catholic missionaries were in perfect fits over what they had seen, Aloysius and Baby were both declaring that when they grew up they wanted to be just like those ladies, and Thackeray had a hard-on (and I don't even think he was disappointed by the lack of nine-year-old boys in tighty-whities.)

"You can certainly see why she's the biggest star in Mexico City," said Candy Bar.

We all nodded in agreement and went to line up outside the dressing room where we found the triumphant ladies of the stage deep in a K-hole, into which we thought we should not intrude. I noticed that there was one figure who a little aside from the mess of semi-nude bodies on the dressing room carpet, and realized that this figure was, in fact, my very own pianist from back in my days at the Diazepam Nite Spot. What a nice surprise! I'd thought he was dead. He'd been working as an auto mechanic since the collapse of the theater and the ensuing financial downturn and had only recently returned to playing music upon his arrival in Mexico City, now that his hands had healed after suffering that merciless blow from a piece of falling plaster back at the cabaret. I couldn't help feeling a little guilty; but whores will have their trinkets, as my grandmother always said, so I asked him on a date.

We took a long walk that wound on for hours. Considering we'd never met before, we had so much to talk about. I didn't know my way around the city, although I'd lived there as long as he had, so he lead me on an endlessly dreamlike voyage under the bridges and over the arches of the place.

We wound up sitting on the riverbank outside the Musée des Beaux Arts, as the sun came up and he asked me to kiss him. Suddenly, I was shy, actually coy and unable to come up with a smart answer. Above our heads, great, big weeping magnolias came into bloom, ripe with fragrance and heavy with want; I took a handful and made him a crown, and he's never since taken it off. Even as the petals droop, the scent is lost to time, the color fades and the flowers turn to dust that powders his hair like icing sugar, he wears it and will wear it right to the grave, which perpetually calls for him.

I lit his cigarette with the oversized lighter bearing the image of a Labrador puppy in a football shirt, which the Statue of Liberty had given me at an Easter picnic. Then, abruptly, unfortunately, it was time to leave, pile back into the car and skid off out of there (Thackeray was fried). Before we even had time to say hello, we said good-bye.

Tearing out of the petrol station and through three lanes of nonexistent traffic, holding my sun hat down on my head, I turned to look over my shoulder at Charlie Chaplin and said, "You know, Charlie, my entire life has been one of sobbing into suitcases."

"Girl, you need to shave," read his card.

In the excitement of Valentino's funeral, I had indeed allowed myself to become peppered with little blue shadows. I simply hadn't had a moment to think about personal hygiene. (I shuddered to think what new and unfriendly visitors had found their way onto and into my body at the Cathedral and imagined the whole car must be swarming with mutating bacteria and alive with microscopic parasites).

As it happened, my paranoid imaginings were curtailed. It wasn't long before we were pulled over close to the border of Monaco by an armed patrol, and I began wondering to myself if we would ever get home, or if, the road was my new home and my life was now one of endless and apparently meaningless incidents. They searched the car, not at all bothered by the fact that Thackeray was crying and screaming and begging them not to arrest him. I don't think the patrol was even affiliated with the police; it was more likely that they were part of the newly devised "Keep Communism out of France" campaign and that they were searching for red propaganda. Luckily, the Catholic missionaries had sold all of their old Stalin memorabilia at a lawn sale in San Diego, or else we could have been in serious hot water. Finding nothing, the patrol presented us with a bomb disguised as a carriage clock and waved us on. With the bomb ticking tartly, we shot off into the twilight of No-Man's land, and on the wind came that distinct voice, calling out, "Diana."

The Tudor manor house in which Thackery's mother was imprisoned was not very much farther. We could see it backlit and bucolic up ahead. Unfortunately, we turned a corner too sharply and hurtled off the road headlong in another motor accident (and there was I promising to never repeat myself).

Falling from a cliff, plunging into the sea, lifestyles of the rich and famous to be ruined by the arrival from above of a banana-yellow convertible right onto their salad Nicoise, upsetting the Perrier and the terriers terribly. Whistling, the air exhaling hard and long against my ears—our ears, I presumed—we approached the rocky, malevolent ground below, and I thought *Oh, Christ! My chance has come at last.* Then I saw Baby and Aloysius flying backward out of the open trunk and into the purple sky. Momentarily they danced on the jet streams of our plunging vehicle. Then gravity caught them by the ankles as she always does, and they plummeted downward themselves.

Certain death is never being certain of anything, and I turned to ask Charlie Chaplin why it was taking so long for us to fuckingwellcrash; but then we hit the ground, bounced around a little and found ourselves in the middle of a rather lovely summer evening barbecue on the beach. Baby and Aloysius fell out of the sky with glee and landed slap-bang in a pile of profiteroles, causing the hostess to scream in delight, "Oh, Harry, you really shouldn't have!"

It was fairly awkward explaining to the hostess that in fact Baby was not her fiftieth birthday present, nor were we, the occupants of the car, a high-end singing telegram service. Charlie Chaplin offered her an autograph as compensation, but it did little to appease her—apparently she was much more of a Buster Keaton fan. We took our leave as graciously as possible, borrowing a few napkins to deal with the various bloody noses and minor nicks and cuts inflicted by our dropping in. By the time we heaved the car back to the highway, it was dark and we were one hundred miles farther away from rescuing Myra; but luckily she was a Pisces and thus terribly patient.

Thirteen

Bouncing along the creepy highway, sleeping in the front seat of that mangled convertible, with the growl of the murder bush trailing us and the insistent ticking of the carriage-clock bomb accompanying my thoughts, for the first half of the night I was terrorized by nightmares. I dreamt that I was trapped in my own body; and recognizing myself to be deep in a dream I screamed for help. I woke myself up and realized that I was not where I thought I was, and thus beyond the reach of the savior I had called out for. For the second half of the night, upon recognizing whom I was sleeping next to, I was besotted by dreams of sex and woke up, sticky. Thackeray later quipped, "Night terrors and wet dreams, that's Diana!"

His mother, Myra, was not easy to rescue. It took gunshots, half a gallon of gasoline and a large box of matches; but we managed it. The Tudor manor where she had been held by her perfidious sister went up in flames, all of its Elizabethan grandness falling amongst the rose gardens and scenic gazebos, walls splitting like dry logs on a pyre, leaded windows melting, drizzling down the facade and crystallizing on all the greedy ivy that coated the building. Thick, acrid smoke billowed as if from a whole village sacked by Vikings, pluming

160

the sky, a great, dirty peacock signaling his lusty demands. We began to choke as we ran down the driveway away from the flaming house and its noxious petroleum fumes, away from the pillaged dining room, pockets heavy with the family silver, away from the cozy living room and the desecrated family splattered around inside, by now no doubt reduced to charred corpses.

There's a certain kind of glee one gets from random acts of ultra-violence inflicted in a domestic setting, I can't describe it any other way. It's exhilarating and not nearly as risky as you might think. I only felt a little disappointed, I suppose, somewhat regretful that it was all so easy, that there was so little at stake, just a few lives. The major loss was, of course, the building itself, with its oak beams and lovely little blue plaque declaring, *Queen Elizabeth I of England slept here*. And she did, too. I know, because I had watched it all on a pirated VHS tape with the Oracle back on the pier in Blackpool. I had seen how she made her presence felt, how she had arrived in 1558 with her backup dancers and a salad bowl full of priceless shimmering stones.

For Good Queen Bess, jewels—great, big, fat emeralds and rubies bloody as a traitor's entrails—were a metaphor for all the things she could not have (would not have), which is to say, heterosexual intercourse and children. Why yes, Bess fucked women by the boatload, and every one would tell you gratefully that her cunt was a regular Aladdin's cave, as bejeweled as any sultan's crown, opalescent and inset with fabulous, fabulous diamonds and pearls. (I remembered a refrain from a song by Prince and the Revolution and made a note to download the audio file at the next militia held service station.)

"Elizabeth," began the missionaries, "Did not screw like a male sex fantasy. She did not beat her bitches and then fuck them with her scepter. No, Elizabeth fucked like a queen in ermine, spoilt, glorious, divine, narcissistic, generous, brave, defiant and hot as a lobster boiled alive."

Baby sighed, "I love this story."

"Good Queen Bess never bore a child, not that she didn't have the capacity; she could have repopulated the country with the fruit of her lusty loins, had it been her will. No, it was a deliberate choice to never take a male lover because she found cum detestable when it spurted towards her. 'I call the shots, sir,' she roared at the Earl of Essex one Christmas morning, when she caught him spunking wildly over the unicorn tapestries—her prized possession, stolen from Nicholas I of Somewhere-or-Other, no less.

"Watching him release his sperm into the air at zero gravity, Liz lost her temper, almost ordered her own execution in her rage (which would, of course, have been treason) and demanded that the Earl get on his hands and knees and clean up the spilt semen with his tongue. She vowed then and there that she would never soil her snowy-white palms with heterosexuality—in fact, she would have made straight sex a crime and a deadly sin, but she was so wired she had misplaced her doomsday notebook and the idea was lost to history.

"'No man shall be the master of *this* Queen!' she bellowed, snapping her fingers and patting her weave; and from thenceforth she took to sexual intercourse solely (in addition to the chicks she had been seducing since kindergarten) with homosexual men, who are not men. She spent her time in her royal gardens pleasuring every queer courtier and bent nobleman she could find; she ate their assholes for lunch and at dinnertime gave them pearl necklaces to wear around Whitehall as a sign of her favor—those were the days.

"She loved her ladies-in-waiting, too. The wives of baronets would positively turn to pools of gelatinous desire when Bess gave them what affectionately became known as *the look*, a look perilously similar to the glare that preceded the frequent and immortal words, 'Off with their head!'

"Good Queen Bess never gave head, no, she only took it; and daily was her rose garden, her gearbox, her dainty truffle and all of her other vaginal metaphors attended to by her devout lovers and their delicious tongues. They say (whoever they are, scandalous gossips) that to have Queen Elizabeth I, Queen of England and Ireland, also known as Gloriana, orgasm on your tongue was to be baptized in honey and awarded the Most Noble Order of the garter. Good Queen Bess' favoring of the noblewomen in her service and their outrageously fey husbands so effeminized the aristocracy that the King of Spain doubled his attempts to conquer Great Britain just to spend a moment in Elizabeth's fabulous pleasure palace.

"He was willing to lay down all his many buckets of gold, his colonies full of priceless spices and even his dentures made from the most exquisite ivory (without which he couldn't say a word) in exchange for just one afternoon listening to disco music at Greenwich Palace with the Queen and her harem, wearing the corset and suspenders he donned in shameful secrecy back in Madrid. But Elizabeth would have none of it. She snorted with contempt when she read His Majesty's begging letters, pleading with her to beat him on the bottom with her scepter. 'You sir (stop) are a highly unoriginal masochist (stop),' she wrote in a telegram to the King, 'and We are displeased above all by lack of imagination (stop).'

"She did not fall for it, no. If she wanted an heir, she would make an heir herself, without the help of any meddling European nonces, thank you very much. If she wanted a son, why, she would simply impregnate one of her ladies-in-waiting herself, with her rock hard cock, for she had one. Elizabeth I, Queen of England and Ireland, Gloriana, was all things to all people, and men wrote her poems in every language known to humankind (and some not) in the hope that she would consider them with the same love and desire she bore for the faggots and nymphomaniacs who swarmed her palaces. But she would not.

"'The trouble with men,' she told the third Duke of Northcumberland as she penetrated him with his crinolines hitched up about his waist and his wife massaged the royal tits, 'is that they think they own the bloody joint. Tell me exactly what kind of X/Y motherfucker is going to beat down my door and make me beg for his dick as though I were a brainless harlot in a pulp novella? This is not *my* first time at the rodeo, of that you can be assured,' she groaned as she rode the Duke to climax.

"'Yes, Majesty, no Majesty, three bags full of oysters and

Jamaican cocoa, Majesty,' moaned the Duke as his brains poured out of his ears with pleasure."

Candy Bar interjected dreamily, "I wish my life was as beautiful as all that."

"Quite," the missionaries agreed and continued, "Lady Northcumberland began guzzling the contents of his head lustily as the Queen immediately (upon climaxing inside the dead man's body) made plans for an elaborate funeral, complete with the naming of a county, a rose and a knot in the late Duke's honor.

"For the next three weeks, awash in sadness that her own libido could kill a man without her prior written consent, Bess sat in the Tower of London crying to herself. She insisted that all the guards pretend that she had been deposed and imprisoned by Mary Queen of Scots, then brought her cousin to trial for the offence. She saw no one, ate nothing, licked deep and long into no blossoming orifices. She spent her time alone sobbing softly to herself, masturbating as she watched the beheadings of rapists, heterosexual men, and other traitors.

"Eventually, washed clean in her tears and her cum, she decided she would also name a sausage after the late Duke, as a final mark of respect, and then thought no more of him."

"Is this going to be a very long story?" interjected Thackeray. "Only I'm low on gas."

"Ahem!" continued the missionaries, with no little hint of indignity.

"Bess set about seducing the late Duke's son, whom she spied applying her very own Venetian ceruse to his face in her very own private chambers, and who she vowed to have as her very own. Startled out of his skin by the sudden appearance of the naked, lithe and terrifyingly beautiful Queen, the young Duke dropped to his knees to beg pardon from Queen Elizabeth I, Queen of England and Ireland, Gloriana, for having invaded her safe space.

"'Worry not,' said Bess, in her falsetto voice, 'we like your face well. The more it likens our face the more we favor it, so please be about your business.'

"She watched him as he whitened his face, blackened his teeth, reddened his cheeks, stepped into her gown, pulled on her wig and set on her crown. The Queen had taken onanism to the most outrageous heights. Liz and her mirror image set upon each other with feverish desire, the beauty of the young boy matched only by the Virgin Queen's mature musculature. Rolling around the rich royal carpets of silk silk silk and ermine, knocking over pewter jugs of sweet wine and crushing fragrant lilies with their passionate cavorting, the two queens became one, ambiguously, giving legendary Castor and Pollox realness, and no one ever could tell them apart. Hidden within her double, Elizabeth was protected against regicide.

"As no one could assassinate Good Queen Bess, no one could force her from her throne before she was ready, before she had completed her mission of bringing the whole of her citizenship en masse into one glowing, sexual om. At the peak of Bess' successes, England looked like a psychedelic rendition of some scene Hieronymus Bosch would have painted, had he a sex drive or a sense of humor. Tongues reached into vaginas and came out of your next door neighbor's mouth only to slide deep into the ears of the weather forecaster, slowly but surely leading the nation to an epochal crescendo of grunts, gasps, heart palpitations, wet patches, record teen-pregnancy statistics, moans of pleasure, record teen-abortion statistics and one all-encompassing orgasm. After which good Queen Bess simply rolled over and died.

"'My work here is done.' "

I wondered why the missionaries had never recorded a book on tape. They had a real flair for storytelling. But with the mansion burning behind us on the horizon and the still sludgy future grimacing before us, it didn't seem the moment to discuss audiobooks, so I regretfully left the subject unbroached.

Myra had been rescued and she was grateful, raving mad, of course, but grateful. We had found the poor woman in a tawdry nightdress and an eye patch, hanging out the tower window, waving a tea towel and singing *Hello, is it me you're looking for?*, shielding her nose from the smoke and the screams that rose up from the massacre downstairs. Charlie Chaplin and Thackeray slung her over their shoulders like a hog ready to roast and bounded out of the house through the fog of atrocious vapors and over the bodies we had mutilated. Outside, recovering, panting, Myra regarded the group of miscreants who had saved her; and then (rather than falling relieved into the arms of her heroic son), the one-eyed prisoner ran over to me, held me close and wept, "You came!"

I was confused.

Pulling herself together for the benefit of the news crews who had assembled on the lawn, as one would expect of an Academy-Award-winning actress, she showered us with the horror of it all. The journalists were frozen with excitement. Myra began her story, claimed she had been kidnapped by her sister, to prevent the Apocalypse. Apparently, Tyra had decided that she quite liked the life she was living out in the countryside with a swimming pool and room for a pony and that she didn't want to give it up. Tyra believed that having a sister who was capable of ending the world was something of a liability, so she locked her up in the granny flat and fed her only shredded copies of *Woman's Weekly*. It was a sort of Edward II scenario, only without the sexy bits. You see, Tyra didn't want to kill Myra (well, not directly), just keep her from doing her job, at least until such time as Tyra decided that life was no longer worth living. Maybe when Tyra lost her looks or depleted the fortune she had made flogging depleted uranium, maybe then, she would have released her sister out into the big, wide world, to end it. Until then, she intended to keep Myra up her sleeve, as her very own cyanide pill, her personal suicide bomber, just in case.

"Unfortunately," said Myra, her voice clear and ringing, striking a powerful note with the ladies and gentlemen of the press, "the prophecy had been written, and no one, no matter how powerful or wicked, can defy the prophecy, not even my dear, late sister Tyra. Just ask King Herod."

The press chuckled amiably.

"For it is written that the world will end, and end it shall! I am the Mother of the Apocalypse! Any questions?"

One journalist asked, "Well, I can't help notice you are wearing an eye patch. This is new, is it not? Is it perhaps the result of some torture inflicted on you by your sister during your imprisonment? Some brutal punishment for having misbehaved in prison?"

"No," she replied curtly. "I gouged the eye out myself with a teaspoon when I saw Bette Davis in *The Anniversary*. I've always admired that woman, such style."

"Couldn't you have simply worn an eye patch without actually plucking out your eye?" the journalist asked impertinently.

"Haven't you ever heard of integrity? Of authenticity? Who did you study with? Do you think Stanislavsky would have said, 'Just fake it, babe'? Well, do you? Cretins! This press conference is over!"

And with that, she turned her back on the rabble of photographers and journalists, who barked, "Myra! Myra! Just one more!" She swept toward us, clasped us together in one encompassing embrace and said, "My babies! Let's split." Streaked with soot, bedraggled but heroic, we asked the press to respect our privacy in this most trying of times. We boarded the car and roared off with our recovering martyr.

From the relative comfort of our overcrowded convertible, Myra recounted the terrible stories of her time locked in her sister's attic. We hung on her every hysterical word, outraged that someone could treat someone they loved as viciously as that. Myra told us how her sister had put her under systematic psychological torture, refusing to allow her visitors or any contact with the outside world, physically abusing her with slaps and kicks, confining her to a wheelchair and even going so far one day as to serve her her own pet canary for lunch.

We were genuinely wet-eyed and dry-mouthed, heart-broken and scandalized by the things Myra was telling us, until Thackeray howled, "Mother, you God damned liar! Those are all scenes from *What Ever Happened to Baby Jane!*" He turned, smacked her full force across the cheek and sobbed, "Is it any wonder I'm such a fucking mess?"

The Catholic missionaries were horrified at the sight of our dear driver slapping his mentally ill mother around. They insisted that he stop the car to apologize; and when he did, they set upon him, forcing him to swallow their spare copy of the Bible, page by bloody page, shoving it, forcing it, cramming it down his throat with wooden spoons and wire hangers. Occasional pieces of his guts were dragged out during the process of force-feeding, slimy slivers and wet tubes that he coughed up, gargling blood and begging his mother's forgiveness. It was not a pretty sight. Baby was shaken, Aloysius repulsed, Myra unconscious, Charlie Chaplin slack-jawed and Candy Bar grimly resigned to the horror, as though she were accepting her fortieth birthday. It's all down hill from here.

I don't think anyone has ever been so glad they had medical insurance as Thackeray was that day. Myra, suddenly concerned, miraculously proactive, woke up and took the driving wheel, and we headed to the nearest Emergency room. This probably ought to be a significant moment in this narrative (Thackeray as passive passenger in his own car, for the first and only time), but it's not; it's more of a coincidental side dish, really. You can think of it as a mixed-leaf salad.

He survived, though we all had to wait five painstaking hours in the duck-egg-blue reception room whilst the doctors pieced him back together as best they could. Hospital waiting rooms, like casinos and submarines, are outside of time, untouched by natural light, ruled by their own laws of passing. Minutes are murdered there in slow agony, and lovers flip their lids, forced to endure the suspense for somewhere between ten minutes and two days—who can say? The great neon highway signs of fate flash on and off intermittently, ALIVE/DEAD, BOY/GIRL, MALIGNANT/BENIGN, THERE WILL BE NO MIRACLES HERE. All around, the jargon of medicine is pitched back and forth as insufferable as a religious conversion or a dietary restriction. Magazines were torn open like sandwiches at a picnic, feverishly, nervously, the whole cast of our motley adventure tossing articles from one to another (we genuinely believed in the power of print); and I had no idea how I had come to be here.

A rage came over me, a genuine white-hot anger that made me want to maim and wound and murder. Who had taken me to the hospital when I was leaking blood and full of my father's semen? Which doctor had sewn me up? Which saint had looked upon me and stemmed my bleeding? Which hero had raised me up, belted me into his SUV and broken the speed limit to get me the help I needed? I wanted Thackeray to die, I wanted to learn the news first and to keep everyone else suspended in gaffa, trapped in the interminable terror of that waiting room for days; an air-conditioned week without sustenance, with only the Klix Cup powdered soup for comfort. And when the truth willed out, I wanted to laugh in their faces as if I had pulled a prank; and I would enjoy their exhaustion, their confusion and their desolation. I would eat up that shit for lunch. Candy Bar could see I was tense.

"I can see you are tense," she said. "Do you want to color with Baby and I?"

I did.

Myra came over to me, looking disheveled and yet somehow projecting a gracious air of poise. There was something terribly familiar about her.

"Are you ready, kid?" she asked me. "We're on soon—we're just waiting on lucky number four, that's all. We have to square off this quadraternity, then we're *on*."

I looked up from my coloring book. I could not tell at all if this woman was a total fruitcake or a prophetess, but she was entirely captivating in her ramblings. Just then Thackeray staggered out of the operating theater, leaning on the arm of his physician, crimson caking the corners of his mouth. No sympathy was on tap, no empathy extended, no explanations or apologies issued. We left rumpled and all wearing pajamas; and upon our exit, as the hospital doors sealed definitively behind us, Candy Bar yelled out in alarm that which we all knew must have been coming.

"The car! Where's the fucking car?"

It had, of course, been stolen.

Such as things are, the hospital sat right on the edge of a lush green forest, which is lucky, isn't it? It was wet with desire and full of booming squawks. We had taken a sizeable detour via hospitals and car crashes to reach it. Presented with two outrageous options, we flipped a coin to decide which way to proceed.

"Heads we walk back to the highway and hitchhike, tails we go through the forest," announced Baby.

The course of true love never did skirt the forest; and it was, of course, tails.

Thirteen

The last time I had seen a forest I was thirteen, on a field trip to look at slugs in their natural environment. As a child I was deeply invested in natural history. I would spend my weekends in the zoological gardens, right up until they were demolished by rebel forces striking back at the revolutionary government.

Caged animals, they said, were counter-revolutionary, and they undertook a national offensive, blowing up more than eighty-five percent of the country's zoos. Many animals escaped, after the detonation shattered their tanks and blew out the walls that held them captive. A pride of shell-shocked lions pounced down Main Street, tearing the throats out of unsuspecting Saturday shoppers, snakes by the hundred crawled out and into suburban homes, flamingos and emus populated local gardens and one hundred thousand locusts set about devouring school children in the yard, picking their bones clean.

Many animals failed to escape; and in amongst the ruins of the zoo, the carcasses of once majestic elephants were found in pools of their own blood. Sharks sprawled and suffocated, rotted in the merciless summer sun. The mangled remains of decimated rhinos littered the walkways of the park.

Necrophiliacs and zoophiliacs picked their way through the treasures, unable to hide their delight at such fantastic good luck, so many fantasies let lose to run amok in the ruins of the zoo.

"This forest stinks of leaves," said Myra.

Baby giggled (she's so inane sometimes).

Deep into the woods, a mile or two or maybe more, Candy Bar confessed her great fear of trees, inspired apparently by the opening scenes of *Snow White*. I had always hated the eponymous Princess. I had always wished that those trees would come to life and chew her up with their jagged mouths. I wished that that very thing would happen right now, to me, to us all, because we deserved it. Instead, Charlie Chaplin, always so keen of hearing though so mute of mouth, noticed a very definite shrieking coming from a deeper part of the forest. He ran toward the sound, dialogue cards that read, *"He needs help!"* trailing him.

"Who?" asked the missionaries, simultaneously.

"Search me," said Baby.

"It's him, it's him! I know it is, it's gotta be, oh, baby, you've come back to Mamma!" Myra raved, running after Charlie.

I for one wanted to sock her but was more than a little afraid of the likely response from the Catholic missionaries. And besides, against my better judgment, I began to be filled with a strange, inexplicably remembered empathy for her and found myself believing her hysterical visions. Well why not?

"We'd better follow them," I mumbled wearily, and we did.

Through the vegetation, onward amongst great vines and purple blooms and thick, twisted creepers, even greener than emeralds, we fought our way, suffocating. Slashing through the foliage into ever-denser plant life, ever-denser darkness, even blacker than the bottom of the sea. Eventually, we broke through into bright light and found ourselves under a sudden tear in the canopy, a wide rip that allowed sunlight to pour in intensely. The sound of shrieking became deafening.

A redheaded boy, very thin, nineteen or twenty, I guessed, was screaming in something approximating fear, or desire. He was so emaciated he could have been a holocaust survivor or a lost traveling salesman; but either way, he was invested with a poignant, mournful sexuality, and the parrots of the forest were sizing him up. Hundreds of brightly colored, almost sparkling, exotically plumed parrots perched above our heads, clustered tightly, quietly on the branches of thousand-year-old Cecropias; and there was no doubt they bore ill will, that their eyes glinted with malice.

"You came!" said the boy. "I knew you would!"

"We came," said Myra, pulling me to her. "Yes, we came."

A surge of recognition rose in my breast. "Freddy?" I called out to the boy quizzically, excitedly. "Freddy, is that you?"

The boy hadn't heard me or chose not to reply. He continued, "Take a look at those parrots, gee whizz."

"I don't know if they want to kill you or fuck you," said Candy Bar, and a shiver seemed to run down her spine.

"Both, I hope," said the boy. "Have my cake and get eaten, too."

Candy Bar sniggered lasciviously. "Both!"

"You know," the boy continued, "it was not far from here that Dostoyevsky's execution took place, or rather didn't. I think that's fitting."

Being a scholar, Thackeray was very taken by the boy and asked him if he had in fact witnessed the event. He whispered his questions to Charlie Chaplin, as he had something of a sore throat, and the words were thus transposed onto dialogue cards. The boy was more than happy to answer; and as he spoke, he stripped himself down to his underwear, whilst eyeing the parrots with anticipation.

So the boy summed up Dostoyevsky's final days.

"Dostoyevsky was arrested for reading flamboyant material; specifically, extreme homosexual pornography, images grossly offensive, disgusting and otherwise of an obscene character. Images are powerful things. They're the physical expression of what lies beneath, an admission that the filth, beauty, horror, and humor of this reality *is* actually visible, though cleverly veiled by priests and advertisers.

When Tsar Nicholas I saw these pictures, he was initially deeply aroused, having only ever seen men in leather, wrist deep in each other's asses, in his dreams. He recognized their halos from the ancient icons hewn in oak and etched in gold throughout the Winter Palace and at first felt overcome with holiness in their presence, sobbing to himself, 'Christ has died, Christ has risen, Christ will come again.'

"He soon sobered up, though, after a short, sharp talk from the Minister of Culture, who informed his Imperial Majesty that, should it become common knowledge that the world really exists, all hell would break lose.

"'As your Highness knows, existence is for the majority a series of repressions, an endless, anecdotal task, a forcing down, a refusal to acknowledge what they see for fear that they are plainly mad. If we allow it to be seen that we all see the same thing, that these visions of violence and brutality, desire and death are not schizoid hallucinations at all, but in fact the strokes that make up the world, well, you can kiss good-bye your mink coats and boy slaves in jockstraps and platinum leashes! If these images circulate, then not even the stupidest, most apathetic fool will be able to continue to convince himself that the world is all Pepsi Cola and God Save The Queen. If they circulate, people will start fucking in the factories and productivity will fall and you'll be out on your ass.'

"The Tsar nodded, growing indignant and recalling the last piece of wisdom Penny Arcade had given him before he sent her to the gulag: *People who don't fuck don't think.*

"'An autocrat,' he announced, 'must have automatic and total control of all images, depictions, explanations and descriptions of everything he rules over. To my subjects I am God, I am dish soap, I am the invention of electricity, I am subsistence, I am eroticized fear and *I am* sex. No one shall go pointing out my hypocrisies and my bad logic. I decide what does and does not exist, and from now on this does not.'

"So Dostoyevsky was thrown into a cell and then dragged back out with two other men and tied to a post in a configuration of three reminiscent of another famous execution. The three men, blindfolded, awaited love letters from the firing squad. But, just as the guards cocked their guns, an envoy arrived, huffing and puffing, declaring that the Tsar had pardoned the men, and two of them promptly went mad on the spot from the shock. But not Dostoyevsky, who, it is said, looked into the mouth of his grave and found her welcoming and comfortable, and thought being ripped away from her arms was the cruelest of all the mockeries in his mock execution.

"But this is how the righteous and just, ordained leaders of the world, ensure that no inappropriate acts are enacted, that no images that portray acts threatening a person's life or likely to result in serious injury to a person's anus, breasts or genitals (not to mention psychological well-being) flow through the flagstone gutters of our minds."

The boy gave a little bow in conclusion and took off his underwear, neatly.

"Amen to that," said Myra, who then fell about laughing, asked if we were on a cruise and if we would be having dinner at the captain's table.

"Who's she?" the boy, now naked, asked of Myra.

"My mother," whispered Thackeray. "She was locked in an attic in a Tudor manor house—it's a Gothic trope."

"Oh, right, I saw the preview for that episode, but I only have a basic cable package so I'm a season behind."

Until then, it had never occurred to me that the cameramen following us were actually filming anything, but I suppose it made sense. After all, there did exist a particularly witty repartee amongst the seven of us—eight if you count the boy, but he was about to die, so we won't.

"This really is the happiest day of my life," sighed the boy, and I noticed that the parrots were circling overhead.

They came in closer, thicker, still silent and without any doubt as to their intent. I stepped toward the boy, too.

"Freddy," I said, my voice fearful and faltering. "Freddy, put your clothes back on, it's cold."

It wasn't cold and he didn't listen; rather, he regarded the ill-natured flock of parrots:

"Eat me or fuck me? Eat me or fuck me?" the boy muttered. "Both."

With that, there descended a frenzy upon him, and those of us who tried to help him were beaten back by powerful, colorful wings and knife-sharp, curved beaks. Parrots rained an erotic carnival down upon the boy, swooping almost lovingly to kiss and to scar him; and the flapping of wings was cacophonous and thunderous, a ceremony announcing the arrival of one giant blue macaw who was to be the father of them all.

With a wingspan equaling that of the boy's outstretched arms, and with a lifespan equaling that of the boy's twenty years, the great blue bird came to the ground evoking nothing if not awe. The boy, now naked, now bloodied, lay on his back in the mud and spread his legs wide apart. With its gargantuan dick, the great blue macaw entered him, penetrated him, sodomized him, buggered him, breached him, fucked him, raped him, owned him. The parrot's enormous penis slid into the boy's butt as deep as the bicep of his first and last boyfriend. He groaned and spat up some blood. The bird rode him, towering over him, and the boy cried out, "Daddy!

Daddy! Daddy!" to the bird, to the forest, to me, to us, to the trees and to the end of the world; and the macaw rode him to a loud climax, screeching like a banshee as it spurted a gallon into the boy's wrecked asshole.

Withdrawing, floating upwards through the tattered canopy, disappearing as a silhouette against the sun, the giant macaw was gone through the hole in the forest canopy; leaving the boy already mortally wounded, blood pouring from both ends of his emaciated body, a new Christian martyr.

We all knew what would happen next, and it did. It unfolded before we could even avert our eyes from the horror of the scene. Every parrot in the forest came down in a wretched mass of feathers, now screaming, and mercilessly set upon the boy, tearing at each other in their bloodlust, dismembering each other in the fight to dismember the dying boy, who didn't even put up a fight. Still lying on his back, the boy uttered not a sound as bird upon bird dropped on him with claws extended and flew off with a beak full of his flesh—a gouged eyeball, savaged fingers, slaughtered ribbons of skin stripped from the bone, bloody mouthfuls of sinew and gristle. Flashes of yellow, streaks of red, belts of green and blue strobed in the throbbing of wings as the boy's body was dismantled with macabre efficiency. When it was done, the parrots ascended, following their father.

I broke away from my companions and ran forward into the twisted mess of feathers and contorted entrails; and tears, actual tears formed at the corners of my eyes as I yelled, "Freddy? Freddy! Oh God, Freddy!" But all that remained of him was his driver's license. Even the pools of blood and the oozy secretions of bile and mucus had been lapped up by the depraved birds, who left nothing behind of Freddy, only the dead and dying of their kind. The organs on the forest floor were theirs, not his; the ground was littered with parrots torn apart, twitching, missing wings and feet and heads, gashed, feathers strewn like confetti, heartbeats fading out. I stood stock still in shock. Candy Bar pulled me out of the nightmare and onto her shaken breast. She smoothed my hair out of my eyes as I whimpered once again, "Freddy."

"I know," she said softly. "Let's leave now."

Without speaking, we all regrouped behind her. "I think we should go this way," she stammered, her arm around my shoulder, leading me on. She didn't know where we were going, but I knew I must go with her. Silently everyone else followed. It was getting dark now, the deeper into the forest we walked, pitch-perfect black, so the Catholic missionaries screwed light bulbs into their empty eye sockets to illuminate our path.

Somewhere in that eternal, silent, steaming-hot forest, with the nauseating murder still fresh in my mind, we came upon a roadside bar with all its chairs upturned on top of its tables. The glare from the eyes of Mercy and Charity lit the scene. Inside, a couple danced though it was late, whilst another couple watched from the sidelines. The dancers moved sexually. She was a good ten years his senior, and both were obviously very drunk, as were their spectators. It occurred to me that the man at the bar was married to the woman on the dance floor, and that she was in fact dancing with the husband of the woman whom her own husband sat alongside.

Love triangles, I lamented softly to myself, and watched as the tensions between the couples rose, until everyone began yelling about somebody's son who had died—somebody's son who had never really existed. We didn't want to watch how the scene unfolded. It seemed inappropriate, in bad taste, one might say. Propitiously the light bulbs in the Catholic missionaries' eyes burnt out with a pop, and we were again alone in the totality of night, a caravan of prophets, all blind now. We walked on, fumbling.

The fear or the wonderment or the flat-out plain lack of comprehension or the sheer exhaustion (who can say?) rendered us speechless. If we ever had had words, we had lost them. If we ever had had knowledge of language, it was gone. Blinded and mute, buried alive in nothingness, doubting our own existence, we walked unwittingly through the forest for hours.

And it stopped just like that.

Neatly, behind a double yellow line (in accordance with zoning regulations), the forest came to a halt, as abruptly as the end of the world. Road markings announced a pristine and, apparently, newly tarmacked slip road, beyond which stood a startlingly upstanding housing estate. Yes, it was that mundane; the sun was rising over an entirely bland landscape, just as she rises over the pyramids of Egypt and the grave of Napoleon.

"Look!" chirped Mercy, pointing to a figure by the roadside. "That's Margaret Thatcher!"

"So it is," said Charity. "The old bitch, she still owes me a fiver."

Sure enough, at the other side of the road, in a royal-blue skirt-suit, stood Margaret Thatcher, thumb in the air, her other hand holding a cardboard sign that read, *Broadway or Bust*.

"Perfect timing," muttered Myra, turning to me maniacally. "There she is," she continued, pulling me close to her crazed visage, "there *she* is."

"I can see that," I intoned, trying to release myself from her grip.

"You know what you have to do," she hissed, with alarming intensity.

I knew no such thing, and I told her so.

"Didn't Beryl make it *clear* enough for you?" she asked mockingly.

I was creeped the fuck out.

"Obviously not," I snapped, and pulled myself free.

Oblivious to my annoyance, Myra continued, "Fucking useless snail! I knew that worthless slug would fuck it up! Never give a snail a man's job, that's what I al ways say!"

She was clearly enraged, and her fists were balled up, but she relaxed them and then spoke to me in a calm but determined manner.

"Do what you came to do, what you promised to do."

I looked at her blankly; her meaning was lost on me. *But then, isn't all meaning lost, now?* I wondered to myself, as Myra's face turned crimson in frustration.

"Take the carriage clock bomb," she said sternly (as though I were a child), "the one the nice gentlemen at the border patrol gave you. Take it and drop it into Margaret Thatcher's bloomers whilst she's not looking. Do it, and end the world. The explosion will trigger Armageddon, *capisce*?"

Candy Bar was standing closely behind me. I could feel her breath on the back of my neck. The Catholic missionaries carried over Baby, who clutched Aloysious in suspense. Charlie Chaplin followed. Sure enough, everyone pulled into a tight huddle to listen to Myra finally unveil the fate of the world, so long cloaked in riddles and the ramblings of snails.

"Do you get it?" asked Myra. "*Comprende?*"

"I'm not sure if I want to do that," I mumbled. "And besides, I left the bomb in the car."

"Yeah," said Candy Bar softly, "that's a bummer."

"Oh, come on, baby!" cackled Myra. "Did you think a little auto theft could stand in the way of Doomsday? Well, did you? I have it right here, ticking away in my handbag."

And sure enough, she did. She produced it with triumphant glee.

"Well, why don't *you* do it, then? Why don't you drop the bomb into Maggie's knickers?" I could hardly believe what I was saying.

"Oh no, baby!" shrieked Myra. "That's not how it's got to be! *You* are the one whose destiny it is—remember the words of the prophecy."

Having never read the prophecy, and feeling at a disadvantage owing to this lack of knowledge, I was suddenly filled with a great remorse for having such a lackluster attitude to attendance at school.

Myra continued, now bellowing, a mysterious rising wind causing her hair to flail around her head. "The Four Horsewomen of the Apocalypse are abroad! Death, Pestilence, War and Famine in that order, if you please! Oh let's be a little less formal, shall we? Really, now, there's no need to stand on ceremony out here by the roadside—nobody's even dressed for dinner! Yes, if we're going to be informal about it, let us say, Diana, Beryl, Myra and Freddy, Death, Pestilence, War and Famine. Diana, Beryl, Myra and Freddy—what a filthy entourage! We could have had our own mini-series, picture it, four single gal-pals living it up in Manhattan on the road to success, dressed to the nines, stuffed with cupcakes and always horny. How different things might have been," she sighed, "but we made a pact, and there's no looking back now—so let's get on with it, then. Don't let us down, Diana!"

Out of thin air, on the disturbed breeze, came the chilling, sensual voice of the murder bush, groaning, as always, slowly and torturously, "Diana," extending my name to three full syllables, "Di-a-na. Di-an-a. Di-an-a. Di-an-a."

I gulped hard, feeling uncomfortable. I was being peer-pressured into eradicating the human race. I looked around me, at my companions, appealing for help, but each face staring back at me was blank, useless, void of any helpful hint and offering no advice. I was sweating, I scanned the sky for a sign, I gazed back into the forest for a clue and perused the horizon; and, to my great relief, I saw a little old Ford Cortina tootling toward us. Surely the driver of such a vehicle would be the type of fellow who could resolve an awkward situation such as this. Undoubtedly he would have a thermos full of tea and some cherry tarts, over which we could discuss what to do next, respectfully and pragmatically.

"Do it! Now!" Myra barked, thrusting the ticking carriage clock into my hands.

Across the road, Maggie Thatcher seemed to perk up a little as she clocked the arrival of the car bumbling along toward her, in no great hurry. She held her flimsy sign above her head with both hands like a political protestor and saucily extended one leg, bending it backward and forward flirtatiously, like a truck-stop tramp (which she was, by the way).

"Hurry!" snorted Myra. "Take the bomb, do it, hurry up!"

And the murder bush's moaning increased in volume and intensity, hissing and crackling all around me like a forest fire of malevolence, "Di-a-na. Di-a-na. Di-a-na. Di-a-na."

The vacant faces of my companions took on a waxy horror-film quality, and the carriage clock ticked noisily, impatiently in my clammy hands.

"Look," I said to Myra, casually, "I don't think I'm up to the job, I...."

She gave me an unceremonious shove toward the road, which shut me up quite promptly. The car came nearer and nearer; by now the radio was audible and playing *Take It Easy* by The Eagles, a classic in anyone's book.

Eyeing Margaret Thatcher and the oncoming, slow-moving Ford Cortina, I spoke up. "You know, I've been through a lot recently, and I don't want to rush into anything like this, without, you know, giving it the proper consideration, I mean, you...."

Taking no prisoners, Myra thrust me full force into the road, causing me to stagger and almost fall on my face. Startled, it took me a moment to regain my balance; and when I did, a wave of outrage overcame me and I entirely lost my temper, with her and with the insistent, increasing cries of the murder bush, repeating my name so endlessly.

"Look lady, who the fuck do you think you are? You better get the fuck out of my face, or so help me God, I will stuff this carriage clock so far down your throat that you'll be shitting cogs! Now, back off, you dumb bitch!"

Myra stood staring at me, slack-jawed. I ran my fingers through my hair, trying to pull myself together, trying to restore a modicum of dignity. I continued, "*As I was saying*, I don't think that the Apocalypse is something we should just rush into, you know?"

As if on cue, the little blue banger pulled up next to Margaret Thatcher. She leaned in through the open window and chatted with the driver; it was the Oracle. Having not once noticed us (nor how close she had come to an explosive demise), Maggie popped open the passenger door and slipped inside. She slung her suitcase into the backseat, where it landed amongst mounds of loose papers, discarded cigarette packets, half-read magazines and a megaphone. She belted herself in and bid the Oracle to drive on. The sweet-natured thing nodded the oracular head and did whatever drivers do with the gear stick to set claptrap old cars in motion. Myra whimpered. As they rolled past us, the Oracle caught my eye, turned the oracular head, and with a very warm smile gave me a little wave of the oracular fingers over the oracular shoulder. Those fingers came up to the oracular lips, brushed them lightly and blew me a kiss.

As the car swerved away down the nacreous tarmac,

Myra howled, then curled up in screams, which quickly died out into sobs and faded into silence. The murmurings of the murder bush gave out in one final long, "Di-an-a," followed by a pathetic, grisly, "Di…" never to be completed, lost on the breeze.

I placed the carriage clock bomb down on the grass; it had stopped ticking. We crossed the road and strolled into the housing estate, perfect, delicate, clean. Mothers on their immaculate front lawns rolled balls softly to their infant sons in romper suits, and fathers in their sports casuals waxed down beaming silver sports cars. Somewhere close by, a barbecue was at work, and elder sisters returned from babysitting the neighbors' kids, dogs barked excitedly and college acceptance letters arrived in the mail for Junior. The scene was strangely, deeply familiar, though I had never experienced anything like it; and nice ladies in Capri pants waved hello to us as we arrived.

Only one garden was unoccupied by busy Sunday families, one garden decorated with a white rose bush, perfectly pruned; sprinklers created water ballets up and down the green grass of springtime. We headed to that garden, thinking that it would be rude not to, and indeed, walked right up the pretty little path and right up to the ajar door; and indeed, straight into the spacious hallway.

Our very own dog barked happily in the backyard. Candy Bar let him come inside and he bounced around with joy, happy to see us again so soon, licking Baby's face; and Baby giggled, *a-coo, a-coo, a-goo, goo, gah*. Inside, the house was exactly as you might imagine, neat, magnolia walls, new but not too new, homely without being worn. It reminded me of someone else's childhood, but I didn't feel as though I were trespassing. Immediately we spread throughout the house, fanned out, full of trepidation, exploring the stillness and the comfortable expanse of the place. I took to the living room and collapsed on the couch, suddenly, finally expended.

Close behind, Baby regarded me with an infantile, maniacal glee, blowing spit bubbles in a manner approaching vicious. Casually, she crawled toward me, as I sat slumped on the glorious upholstery of that three-seat settee, slightly distracted by the quietude of this strange new place and somewhat put on edge by the presence of a *living* dog on the premises. Stealthily, murderously, Baby pulled herself up onto my legs, steadied herself and fumbled a sneeze. With strength unnatural for her size, she pried my legs apart; and though I tried to force them closed again, I couldn't, because I was overpowered.

"Now, Baby," I said in a firm maternal tone, "don't be rude. That isn't nice."

She offered me no reply, and I felt panicked. I wondered, *If I begin to shriek, would anyone here help me?* No. No one would have helped me. Baby stared between my splayed legs, regarded my cock and balls with disdain but was not discouraged. Baby was going home.

Since she could no longer crawl into my cunt, lost as it was on the roadside somewhere in Idaho, Baby had to think outside the box. Like the angel rolling away the rock from the mouth of Christ's tomb, she lifted up my balls; she felt underneath me to find my asshole, balled up her hand and with a tiny fist began to punch her way inside me. Something wet and viscous poured out of me (I think it was Crisco); my ass was self-lubricating with palm oil. Moments of great trauma, right? First with one, now, with two arms up to the elbow, Baby distended my hole, pushing out against the adverse, constricting pressure and forcing her head inside me like a diver breaking the surface of the water. I gasped; a gust of air rushed inside me, causing me to inflate momentarily as Baby's shoulders took shelter.

I didn't hurt, it wasn't agony. As Baby entered me, I felt only the mild embarrassment of watching a young child do something inappropriate for which one knows not how to chastise her. I relented, let my muscles go lax; Baby was in me, as deep as her clavicles. From then it was easy; the width of her tiny body tapered down to her miniature feet, one of which dangled briefly outside my sphincter after my hole closed quickly around her with an ungracious squelch. I was pregnant again; and from the doorway, Candy Bar watched proudly (she would make an excellent father).

I heard the gentle padding down the carpeted stairs of the Catholic missionaries returning from exploring the bed-rooms upstairs. Leading his crestfallen mother by the hand, Thackeray returned from investigating the wonders of the kitchen, spackled with mustard. Charlie Chaplin, clutching Aloysius and a toothbrush, looked satisfied with his recon-naissance trip to the bathroom. Settled together in the living room, someone, I'm not sure who, switched on the TV. In-comprehensible sounds and pictures poured from it, grin-ning, inane, terrifying in close-up, acid-bright, hysterical, psychedelic babbling. It was a shampoo commercial, and we all turned our attention to it.

The End

About the Author

British-born, American-educated Berlin resident La John-Joseph is a performance artist and writer. The original scriptwriter for radical Californian Dada drag revue, BoyfriendRobotique, he is also a librettist and the author of the critically acclaimed solo memoir play *Boy in a Dress*. Her performance work has taken him from the San Francisco MOMA to the Royal Opera House, and across Europe, the USA and into the middle East. His short fiction has appeared in numerous anthologies and zines, including *The Gay Times Book of Short Stories*, *Bird Song*, *P.S. I Love You*, *Fat Zine*, and *21st Century Queer Artists Identify Themselves*. *Everything Must Go* is her first novel.

Made in the USA
Charleston, SC
18 February 2015